BLIZZARD OF LOVE

A LONG VALLEY WESTERN ROMANCE NOVELLA - BOOK 2

ERIN WRIGHT

WRIGHT'S ROMANCE READS

To my own cowboy:
Thanks for not making me move to Arizona. You know I'd
rather be cold than hot any day of the week.

CHAPTER 1

LUKE

DECEMBER, 2016

*L*UKE NASH WANDERED down the aisle of Frank's Feed & Fuel, looking for a new halter for his mare. He didn't *need* a new halter, of course – he had a half dozen for her already – but dammit all, he was tired of being holed up at home. Usually, he could go weeks at a time out on his farm, ignoring the outside world, but lately, he'd started getting antsy.

It was probably because Christmas was coming, the most hated time of the year. The music, the bells, the lights, and worst of all, the fake cheerfulness that just meant that someone was trying to sell something to him. It was a sham, a marketing scheme.

And yet, how did he escape it? Shopping, with his dog no less, two days before Christmas.

It was like a cruel joke played on him by the universe.

With a sigh, he dismissed the halter choices and wandered over into the hardware department to eyeball new cupboard handles. Maybe he should remodel his kitchen this winter. That would give him something to do. Countertops and cupboard handles would make a world of difference to how his kitchen looked. He could—

"Hey, Luke!"

The greeting broke into his thoughts, startling him, and he whirled around to see his best friend, Stetson Miller.

"Did I give you a heart attack?" Stetson said, grinning.

"Oh hell, if Carmelita doesn't stop feeding you cinnamon rolls every morning, she's going to be the one giving you a heart attack," Luke volleyed back. Carmelita was Stetson's housekeeper/cook extraordinaire, a surrogate mother after Stetson's mom died when they were in junior high.

And based on the roundness of Stetson's stomach, it looked like she was trying to fatten him up like a Christmas goose.

"Damn, you should see Jennifer," Stetson said. "She's fattening up *real* nice."

Luke bit back his grin. He was pretty sure Stetson's pregnant wife would *not* be happy if she heard her husband say that.

"So, what are you and ol' Willie doing for Christmas?" Stets asked.

Luke just stared blankly at him for a moment. *Doing* for Christmas? That made it sound like he was going to go out caroling or something. And with ol' Willie to boot. The idea of his crusty, old farmhand singing Christmas songs was ridiculous, and Stetson knew it.

"What if you headed over to my house for the weekend?" Stetson continued when Luke didn't — couldn't — say anything. "Might as well take advantage of the fact that Christmas is on a Sunday this year. Carmelita would love to have someone else to hover over and cook for."

Luke contemplated a whole weekend of Carmelita's cooking — hams and gingerbread cookies and mashed potatoes and oh God, *pies* — against the idea of actually having to celebrate Christmas this year, instead of just treating it like any other day of the year.

His stomach rumbled, reminding him that he hadn't eaten anything but a piece of toast with peanut butter on it all day. Well, toast and lots and lots of coffee.

Stetson heard the rumble and laughed. "I'm going to take that as a yes. Come over as soon as you can. I'll tell Carma to set another plate at the table." Without waiting for a reply, he turned and headed for the cash register, a roll of copper wire in his hands.

Luke stared at his retreating back for just a

moment, sighing in an odd combination of frustration and humor, and then snapped his fingers. Sticks, his black lab, headed back towards him from where he'd been alternatively sniffing and then licking the dog food bags. "Come on, boy, let's go get our stuff. You get to guard the Miller farm this weekend." Sticks wagged his tail with delight and trotted along behind Luke, his toenails clicking on the floor as they went.

Luke was only a little bit surprised that he'd somehow been shanghaied into spending Christmas with Stetson, without ever giving his consent to the idea. Stetson was a force of nature, and worse yet, he knew that Luke had nothing to go home to, no one to please. He knew the truth about Luke's pathetic life, and so Luke couldn't even offer socially acceptable white lies about being too busy to come over.

Dammit, sometimes it was a pain in the ass to have a best friend who knew him so well. Sticks jumped into the bed of the truck and Luke gave him a quick pat on the head before sliding into the cab.

It was time to go pack some clothes and then go eat Stetson out of house and home. At least he could exact his revenge on Stets for his high-handedness that way. Served him right.

CHAPTER 2

BONNIE

ONNIE PATTERSON WALKED into the house, her arms full of purchases. Without her family in town for Christmas, she'd had shockingly few people to go Christmas shopping for this year, so she'd ended up shopping for herself instead. She now had a new lamp for her nightstand, a shower curtain for the bathroom, and an adorable red peacoat, all curtesy of the thrift store. She couldn't afford shopping elsewhere, and anyway, she *liked* the hunt – the thrill of finding something great in amongst all of the junk.

Her phone began vibrating in her pocket and, after pulling it out and checking caller ID, swiped to the right and shoved it between her shoulder and cheek.

"Hey, Jennifer!" she said enthusiastically as she began unloading her bags. "It's been so long since we've talked – I was just thinking about how much I missed you. How's it going up in Sawyer?"

Jennifer, her closest friend in the world, had married some cowboy just a couple of months earlier and had moved to Long Valley of all places, some tiny podunk corner of the world where people still honest-to-God canned their own food every fall and *intentionally* listened to country music. It was a world that Bonnie couldn't help catching a glimpse of occasionally, living in Boise, Idaho as she did, but still, Sawyer just seemed so…quaint.

The kind of thing you saw on a postcard but didn't think still really existed.

Well, not in *real* life.

"Awww…" Jennifer said, a smile in her voice. "I've missed you, too. Things have been awesome up here. Things are starting to settle down now that harvest is done. You can't grow anything in a foot of snow!"

"A foot?" Bonnie repeated, stunned. Surely she was kidding. There was only a skiff of snow on the ground outside Bonnie's apartment, and Sawyer and Boise were only 90 minutes apart. How was it possible that so much snow had fallen up there?

"Yeah, I think it's snowed more up here in the last month than it did all last winter in Boise. I really like it right now; you'll have to ask me in February if I still feel that way or if I'm starting to go a little snow-crazy." She laughed and Bonnie couldn't help smiling in return. It was amazing how much better the world seemed with Jennifer in it. "How's work going?"

"Ugh," Bonnie groaned, and then laughed. "About that good. I can't believe you and I worked so hard to get our degrees in accounting so we could be this miserable at work. Well, so *I* could be so miserable. How're you doing with the handsome hubby?"

"Good!" The love and cheerfulness in Jennifer's voice rang through and Bonnie knew Jenn meant it. Of course, she was married to a drop-dead gorgeous cowboy and no longer had to put up with a boss from hell, so Bonnie supposed that she was genuinely just that happy.

Lucky.

"Anyway, are you doing anything fun with your family for Christmas?"

Bonnie grimaced, glad her friend couldn't see her expression. "No," she said, struggling to keep her voice light and airy, while lying for all she was worth. "Mom and Dad – well, Mom, and then Dad went along with it because he wanted to make her happy – decided to take everyone and go to Hawaii for Christmas. Palm trees and walks along the beach just doesn't sound Christmassy to me, so I opted out of the trip."

Bonnie was pretty sure lightning was going to strike her apartment for such a blatant lie, but was surprised when nothing happened. Maybe God wasn't paying attention to her just then, which probably just as well. She wasn't sure if she had lightning strikes for lies in her rental insurance coverage.

"Oh Bonnie, I'm so sorry to hear that. Listen, why don't you come up here? Sawyer has plenty of pine trees and craggy mountains, so I'm pretty sure it passes your 'Must look Christmassy' test. It's been a week since the last snowstorm, so the roads are all cleared now and anyway, I'm sure Stetson and Carmelita would love having someone else here for Christmas."

"Really? I wouldn't be an imposition?"

"Of course not! Wyatt can't come for Christmas, of course, and Declan is mad at Stetson for not being more forgiving, so it was just going to be Stetson, me, and Carmelita for Christmas. The little one isn't due until April, so we can't count on that quite yet." She laughed. "You should come up tonight and spend the weekend here. Take advantage of the fact that Christmas is on a Sunday. Do you have Monday off too?"

"I do – even Boss McScrooge agreed that there was no client on the planet who would be demanding numbers on December 26th."

Jennifer's joyful laughter spilled out of the phone's speaker. "Well, maybe you should upgrade him to Boss McScrooge Lite just for that."

"Let's not get crazy," Bonnie grumbled as she tried to fight back her own laughter. Jenn could always make her grin. Ever since they met in the Survey of Federal Income Taxation class, which sounded as awful as it really was, they'd been drawn together – a perfect match of fun and laughter. Jennifer had moved in soon afterwards, living on Bonnie's couch for two years while they worked their way through Boise State University to get their degrees.

It was how Jennifer had managed to escape from Paul, her ex and a man so vile, Bonnie never could understand Jenn's attraction to him.

Not everyone has the benefit of hindsight. And hey, she doesn't make fun of you for Ryan, so...

"Yay! Pack quickly and head over. See you in a couple of hours?"

"Sounds good. See you soon." Bonnie hung up and hurried to get her bags packed. It was time to go have some fun, and get the hell out of her apartment.

CHAPTER 3

LUKE

*L*UKE PULLED UP in front of the old Miller farmhouse, the Christmas lights that were lining the roofline sparkling in the snow covering the landscape. It looked so festive, so Christmassy and shit.

So unlike his own house.

Sticks jumped down from the bed of the truck, his stocky Labrador body navigating the snowdrifts with ease. Luke and Stick's noses wiggled in the crisp night air, breathing in the smell of…was that pot roast?

God, it's gonna be nice to eat Carmelita's cooking this weekend. I might end up as fat as Stetson when she's done with me! Oh, but it'll be worth it.

He knocked once and then, brushing his feet on the welcome mat, pushed open the front door. "I'm here," he called out. Sticks shook the snow off his fur and then trotted in behind him.

"Hello!" Carmelita came bustling into the entryway, the delicious pot roast and...something else trailing in behind her, like the world's best smelling perfume. *Is that cinnamon rolls? I'm pretty sure it's cinnamon rolls.*

His stomach rumbled its agreement.

"Oh, you poor thing," Carmelita said in her heavily accented English, taking his jacket and hanging it up in the hall closet. "Dinner will be done soon. You go upstairs and I will tell Stetson and Jennifer you are here."

She bustled off before he could answer, and so he headed up the stairs and down to the far guest bedroom. It was a little less...girly and shit than the other one, so it was the one he usually chose when he spent the night at the Miller's house.

He lay down on the bed for a few minutes, closing his eyes and turning the idea of doing absolutely nothing for an entire weekend over and over again in his mind. This was something he hadn't done in years. Was he even capable of doing nothing for an entire weekend? He didn't know.

Dammit, am I really only 26 years old? I sound like an old man. Time to stop wallowing in my geriatric ways and get moving.

He decided to take a quick detour to the bathroom before heading downstairs, but when he slid the pocket door open, he saw something that he was pretty sure he'd never, *ever* forget: A half-naked woman, jeans down around her knees, and the most sexy pair of red lace underwear on that he'd ever seen.

It was only then that he registered a screaming noise, and realized it was because of him. She was screaming at *him*.

A whole lot of not-very-nice words.

CHAPTER 4

BONNIE

*B*ONNIE HAD SOFTLY HUMMED *We Wish You a Merry Christmas* on the way up the stairs. Jenn had told her to use the first guest bedroom on the left at the top of the stairs because it was simply gorgeous – she'd promised hand-painted roses on the walls, a fireplace, and a beautiful canopy bed, which sounded heavenly. Who *actually* had a canopy bed?! Her inner princess was squeeing with excitement.

When Bonnie opened the door, she gave a drawn-out sigh of appreciation, a smile spreading across her face. Jennifer hadn't been exaggerating. The room was too beautiful to use.

On second thought, it was too beautiful *not* to use.

With a big grin, she placed her bag on the bed and then headed to the sliding pocket door on the far side of the room. She'd use the bathroom before she headed back down the stairs to find the source of that amazing smell that was wafting through the house.

She was almost to the toilet, her jeans around her knees, her thumbs in the waistband of her panties, *when a stranger walked into the bathroom.*

She was screaming and trying to pull up her jeans that'd somehow gotten tangled around her knees and then she was pitching sideways into the clawfoot bathtub and her screams were reverberating around in the tub, hurting her head, or maybe that's because she'd hit her head on the lip of the tub when she'd fallen that was causing her head to throb and *the stranger was still there*, his lips moving but she couldn't understand anything he was saying and then his red plaid shirt appeared above her, a towel in his hands and he was draping it over her lower half and backing slowly out of the bathroom, hands in front of him, never turning his back on her until he'd backed out of his pocket door into his bedroom, sliding the door closed quietly as he disappeared from sight.

After countless moments, she could finally breathe again and the screaming stopped and she panted, staring at the ceiling. She reached up and felt the knot on the back of her head, wincing when she pushed on it.

At least I didn't split my head open! Oh my God, who was that man?!

Based on his cowboy hat and plaid shirt, she was pretty sure he was a local, which meant he had to be a friend of Stetson's. She tried to think back to Jennifer and Stetson's wedding day, to remember if she'd seen him then, but it'd been a wild day and there'd been a whole lot of cowboys in attendance.

A full-body shiver ran through her, a reminder that she hadn't managed to pull her jeans back up yet, and lying inside of a cast-iron tub probably wasn't the warmest place in the house to hang out.

With some very unladylike maneuvering that she was eternally thankful she didn't have an audience for, she managed to get her jeans pulled back up. With a sigh, she shoved her hair out of her face and clambered out of the tub. She could hide all night in the bathroom and hope Voyeur Cowboy went away, or she could go downstairs and pretend that nothing happened.

Absolutely nothing at all.

She straightened her shirt and her hair before heading down the stairs to join what promised to be the world's worst dinner party.

She walked into the living room just as the cowboy-turned-voyeur said, "And then, she fell over backwards into the tub!"

Stetson roared with laughter, Jennifer whacked him upside the head, and then, dammit, a strangled noise escaped Bonnie's throat which made everyone turn and look at her, the absolute last thing she wanted in the world but she couldn't pretend she hadn't heard the conversation now, and so, righteous indignation flaring up inside of her, she advanced on the Cowboy Without Manners.

"Why did you not knock before you came in?" she demanded. "Were you raised in a barn?"

"Ummm…kinda."

She glared at him but before she could tell him *exactly* what she thought of his manners, Stetson broke in.

"So, you two have met?" he asked dryly.

She turned and glared at him. Really, two boneheads in a room at a time was more than she could handle. *Shouldn't there be some sort of load capacity rule in place?* Before Bonnie could whack him across the head and tell him exactly what she thought of him – thought of both of them – Jennifer pulled her to the side. "I'm really sorry for this. I—"

"Are you trying to set me up with that…that man?" Bonnie demanded. Suddenly, it all made sense. She was supposed to be spending Christmas with one of her closest friends and now, some Peeping Tom cowboy was thrown into the mix. "Because if you are, let me tell you right now, he is *not* my type!"

"No, I promise, it was just a mixup. Stetson asked him to come this weekend and I asked you, and we hadn't talked to each other yet, so we didn't know. We figured it out about the time, well, that you—" She gestured helplessly with her hands, a smile quirking up on the edge of her lips, threatening to spread across her face, and Bonnie narrowed her eyes at her. Jennifer's grin quickly disappeared.

"Right about the time you had an unwanted

visitor in your bathroom," Jennifer finished quickly. Bonnie felt her righteous indignation start to melt away, and laughter slowly replace it. *Not* that she'd let it show on her face. Hell no. She was going to make them all squirm for a while. A long while.

Okay, so the whole thing *was* damn funny, and in about 15 years, she might even laugh about it.

"I'm sorry," Stetson said, walking over to their little huddle in the corner. "I was the one who asked him about the sounds. It was…quite noisy." His lips quirked, and she could tell he was fighting back laughter, too.

She glared daggers at him and his laughter dried up as quickly as Jennifer's had. Turning on her heel, she stalked into the dining room but then stopped when she realized she didn't know where to sit at the large, imposing table. Jennifer came to her rescue, such as it was – Bonnie ended up sitting across the table from Voyeur Cowboy, which she wasn't sure was any better than sitting next to him.

Ugh. She wasn't sure what the seating arrangement should be, but she did know she hated this one. They began passing the dishes around the table, the silence awkward as hell.

"So, how did you and Jennifer meet?" Stetson knew the answer to his question, but Bonnie gave him credit for trying to come up with a topic to break through the seemingly impenetrable silence that had blanketed the room. Voyeur Cowboy stared at her across the table, also waiting for her answer, dark brown eyes following her every movement.

Like melted chocolate.

She ignored that thought.

"We both went to Boise State, and met in the Survey of Federal Income Taxation, a class from hell. We needed study partners, so…" She shrugged. "Then she broke up with her ex and needed some place to live, so she moved in with me for two years."

Voyeur Cowboy watched her as she talked and she dropped her gaze to her plate. She shouldn't let him get to her, but it was hard not to notice his chiseled jaw, or his lightly stubbled cheeks. It was quite possible she could cut herself on those cheekbones.

"I'm sorry, I never caught your name," she said to Voyeur Cowboy, when it became obvious that no one was going to actually introduce them.

"Oh!" Jennifer exclaimed. "I'm so sorry. Bonnie Patterson, this is Luke Nash. Luke, Bonnie. He's Stetson's best friend."

"How did you and Stetson meet?" she asked, the words leaving her mouth before she could catch them, pull them back and hide them away. She was supposed to be giving him the cold shoulder, dammit, not asking him questions. He smiled at her, the edges of his eyes wrinkling into deep crow's feet, and she wondered how old he was. He seemed timeless.

His hair is still dark, but maybe he dyes it.

Dammit, Bonnie, he's Voyeur Cowboy. No wondering about

his age, or how he met Stetson, or if you really could cut yourself on his cheekbones.

Cold.

Shoulder.

"Oh hell, Stetson and I met while we were both still in the womb," he said, winking at her. She stared back at him blankly.

"Our moms were good friends for a while, so they hung out together while pregnant," Stetson jumped in, sensing her confusion. "Of course, I am the older and wiser of the two of us—"

"—Only by two months!" Luke broke in.

"—So *obviously* I got the good looks too," Stetson finished, ignoring his friend's huff of pretended indignation. Jennifer swatted at Stetson's arm.

"You be nice. Poor Bonnie here is going to think that you treat all of your friends this way."

"That's 'cause he does," Luke grumbled.

She couldn't help it – she laughed. Just a small laugh but it spilled out of her before she could stop it.

All right, maybe just give him a slightly cold shoulder, instead of an ice-cold shoulder. After all, Momma raised me to be nice to everyone, even assholes who don't deserve it.

Carmelita bustled into the dining room, bearing a tray with small dessert plates arranged on it.

"Cinnamon rolls for everyone for tonight," she said cheerfully as she distributed a plate to each person. Bonnie stared at the dessert set down next to her dinner plate, her eyes wide.

Oh man, if I'd known this was coming, I would've eaten less pot roast!

As everyone dug into their cinnamon rolls, the topic drifted back to Paul, Jennifer's ex, and the visit he'd made to Stetson's house that summer.

"And then, he started threatening me that he'd call the sheriff on me!" Stetson laughed, which caused Luke to laugh also, a strangely rusty sound that…she liked more than she ought to.

It took her a moment to put meaning to Stetson's words. "Hold on, why is that funny?" she asked, confused.

"'Cause the sheriff goes hunting out here each fall," Luke said, as if that explained everything. She just stared at him. Again.

"Out here, you don't mess with the people who let you go hunting on their private property," he continued when it became obvious she had no idea what his statement was supposed to mean. "Stetson doesn't have to give permission to anyone to go hunting out here, so if the sheriff wants to continue to get good access to deer and elk, he isn't likely to piss off Stets. I mean," he shrugged nonchalantly, "I doubt the good sheriff would allow Stetson to murder someone and just get away with it 'cause he wants to go hunting, but is he going to believe the word of some blustery fool over Stetson? Hell no."

Stetson laughed. "Yeah, that look on his face was priceless. It was pretty damn fun to pick him up and chuck him into that puddle, I have to admit. And then after that…" He turned and looked at Jennifer, and the heat arcing between them had Bonnie blushing. It was obvious that they were deeply in love, and a pang of longing shot through her.

Someday, I'd love to have someone look at me like that. Someday…

CHAPTER 5

LUKE

*L*UKE AWOKE IN A PANIC, jackknifing into a sitting position. He'd slept in! He'd better get up and get the horses fed. They were probably starving by now. And—

Oh. Right. I'm at Stetson's house. For Christmas. On vacation.

Several different concepts that were completely foreign to him.

His nose twitched. Hold on, was that bacon *and* pancakes? He hopped out of bed, sucking his breath at the icy floor beneath his feet, and hurried into his clothes. If Carmelita had made breakfast, there was no way he was going to be late getting downstairs.

He thought back to the night before as he headed down the stairs. Was Bonnie going to continue holding it against him that he'd walked in on her? He just hadn't expected to be sharing the guest bathroom with someone else, *especially* not a female. It hadn't occurred to him to knock, although he regretted his smart-aleck response to her rhetorical question about being raised in a barn.

Wasn't there something about how you should stop digging when you're already in over your head?

"…never done it before," Bonnie was telling Stetson as Luke walked into the dining room. There was a spread on the sideboard to make a grown man cry, and as Luke listened to the discussion, he was busy loading up his plate with scrambled eggs, pancakes, bacon, sausage, and homemade biscuits. He was pretty sure he couldn't eat everything, but he also knew he couldn't keep himself from loading up on it anyway.

"Well, I'm good friends with another rancher who has a patch of land that he's kept in timber. I'll go call him and see if he'll let us wander through today."

"What are we wandering through the forest for?" Luke asked, sliding into his seat at the table. Bonnie was sitting across from him again this morning, her hair tousled, her cheeks flushed from sleep.

Damn, she's gorgeous.

He stopped that thought right there. Absolutely *no* reason to continue down that rabbit hole. A city girl and him were a good idea, just like setting his house on fire would be a good idea.

"Bonnie here has never chopped down a Christmas tree before," Stetson said, as if declaring that she'd just recently wriggled out from underneath a rock to plop herself down at his dining room table.

Luke stared at her and she just shrugged. "It's easier to put up a fake tree every year."

A…fake…tree? His mind turned the words over and over again, as if trying to understand a new language, and then gave up on the concept.

What did you expect? She's a city girl, through and through, which is why you made the "Yeah, kinda" comment yesterday in the middle of her yelling at you. You can't help yourself. Needling city girls is an Olympic sport at this point.

"Well, I think it's about time we pop your real-Christmas-tree cherry," Luke said, smirking at her. She gasped and then narrowed her eyes at him, opening up her mouth to give a stinging retort…just as Carmelita bustled in with a coffee pot.

"I will not have that kind of language here," she said mildly as she refilled Stetson's mug, stroking him absentmindedly across the shoulders as she moved around him. Bonnie grinned at Luke triumphantly as Carmelita walked past him, coffee pot in hand, ignoring his empty coffee cup.

Dammit, I need to remember Carmelita's filter on language is a little more stringent than mine. When am I going to stop shoving my boots in my mouth?

His mom had always told him his smart-aleck mouth would get him in trouble one day. Well, "always," as in before she up and abandoned him and their whole family. After spending years whining about living in the Middle of Nowhere, as she'd christened Sawyer, she'd gotten stuck one night, trying to get out of the driveway. The snow drifts were high

– it was Christmas Eve, after all, and there'd been snow on the ground for a couple of months by that point – and she'd skidded off into the ditch several times before Luke and his dad could get the car pointed in the right direction.

Cursing, she'd slammed her car door and took off down the driveway, her red taillights brilliant in the dark and bitter cold. She was just going to go get some milk.

Years later, and still no milk. Luke hadn't seen his mother since that night.

He wouldn't touch milk. It was his own silent protest against the injustices of the world.

Now, he was facing yet another city girl – another woman who thought that roughing it was when her iPhone got four bars of service instead of five.

She may've won this round, but she wouldn't win the war.

Jennifer came stumbling in, her hair mussed, her PJs askew, her belly starting to round beneath her top.

Stetson is a damn lucky guy.

Luke made himself stop right there. The last thing he was going to do was covet his best friend's wife. He hadn't been to church in a while, but even he remembered that commandment.

"Did I hear Christmas tree talk?" she asked around a wide yawn.

"Yup – we were talking about going up to Colt's place and chopping one down for the living room."

"Oh good!" she said, her enthusiasm temporarily

outweighing her yawns. "It's been bothering me that here we are, the day before Christmas, and still no tree in the house. It's just been so crazy with everything happening…" She sat down with a plate overflowing with food, and Carmelita bustled back in to fill her coffee cup.

She ignored Luke's empty mug again, and he realized with a sigh that the coffee he'd managed to drink thus far was all he was going to get for the day.

They finished the meal, the conversation ebbing and flowing like the tides. Despite the missing coffee, Luke was enjoying the hell out of the meal. He usually made a pot of coffee in the morning and then headed out to the fields to work. A lavish breakfast like this was…unheard of.

It wasn't long before they headed out the door, jumping into Stetson's four-door pickup and driving up into Colt's place. Sticks was in the bed, his head sticking out the side, ears flapping in the wind. Sticks refused to get into the cab of a truck; his place was the bed and that's where he was going to be, dammit. Luke used to worry about him getting cold but if he ever was, he didn't show it.

"Man, those clouds don't look good," Jennifer said, peering through the windshield towards the Goldfork Mountains. There was a storm front coming in, dark and ominous clouds moving steadily over Long Valley.

"I'm trying to pull up the weather app to see what we're looking at, but I can't get the page to load,"

Bonnie said, staring at her phone in irritation. Stetson glanced at her in the rearview mirror.

"I watched the news this morning," he said reassuringly. "It looks worse than it is. We're only supposed to get about an inch of snow from the storm. 'Round here, that's nothing."

"Oh," she said, surprised. Luke couldn't help it – he actually agreed with the city girl. It didn't look like a one-inch-of-snow kind of storm to him, either. "Thanks. I'll stop worrying about it then." She turned off her phone and set it off to the side, something else that surprised him. He thought if she wasn't messing with the weather app, she'd be scrolling through her Facebook app or taking a selfie or something else equally obnoxious.

Jennifer turned up the radio and began singing along lustily to the Christmas music.

A beautiful sight
We're happy tonight
Walking in a winter wonderland

Laughing, Bonnie and Stetson joined in. Luke kept himself from rolling his eyes, but only barely. How did these people actually like Christmas? It was a concept that seemed…impossible to him. Christmas was jangling music and people buying presents they couldn't afford for people they didn't like and…

And mothers leaving their three children to fend for themselves, with only a mostly absent father to occasionally try to fill the void.

Luke pushed the thought of his mom away, just

like he always did. This time of the year just tended to bring up her memory more often than usual, was all.

The switchbacks finally ended and they pulled off into a wide spot in the road. They all clambered out of the truck, Stetson pulling two hand-axes out of the bed of the truck and handing one over to Luke before they set off traipsing through the woods, Sticks following along behind.

Luke grumbled as he swung the ax over his shoulder. "What's up with the hand axes? Are we pretending chainsaws haven't been invented yet?"

Stetson shrugged. "Jennifer said axes would be more romantic." When Luke rolled his eyes so hard, he was afraid they were in imminent danger of falling out of his head, Stetson just grinned unrepentantly. "Wait until you're married. Oh, how the mighty falls. You're gonna find yourself doing all sorts of stupid-ass shit, like chopping down a pine tree with an ax."

Luke couldn't help laughing. The idea was just preposterous. He glanced at the two women trudging through the snow, Bonnie's snow pants a little too tight across her hips because she'd tried to squeeze into a pair of Jennifer's, and caught his breath.

All right, fine, so maybe there's some things I might be willing to do to get a female into bed. But chopping down trees by hand isn't one of them!

"Stets!" Jennifer shouted, glancing back at them, her cheeks flushed red by the cold and exertion from wading through the snow. She was beaming from ear to ear. "I found it!"

Luke looked at the tree she was pointing at, and grudgingly admitted that *if* they were going to pick a tree to stick inside of a house, that was the tree to pick. Tall, straight, and full, it looked like it'd jumped right off a Christmas card.

"It's perfect," Stetson said as they stopped next to it, everyone admiring for a moment.

Even Luke, although he wasn't going to admit it out loud.

"Ready?" Stetson asked him, grinning, and they began formulating a plan of attack on the tree, trying to figure out the easiest way to fell it and drag it back to the truck. Jennifer and Bonnie began wandering off, looking for "Christmas greenery" as they put it, although Luke was damn sure there was no ivy growing in this forest.

Well, maybe poison ivy.

Stetson and Luke began hacking away at the tree, the thunks of the ax strikes ringing through the cold, thin air. Luke could hear the girls giggling over something off behind him, but he didn't pay much attention to them. He was starting to get into a rhythm, his arms swinging without conscious thought guiding them.

Bored, Sticks wandered off into the trees, and then his happy bark started echoing back, telling Luke that he was finding a rabbit or two to chase through the snow. Sticks was dumber than a rock and would never catch a rabbit, but that didn't keep him from trying again, and again, and again.

Just as they were getting close to the end, the wood crackling under the pressure of gravity, Luke saw movement out of the corner of his eye. Bonnie and Jennifer had wandered right into the fall zone of the tree.

"Watch out!" Luke yelled, throwing his ax to the side and hurrying through the deep snow as quickly as he could. The women glanced up as he bore down on them, surprise and shock lining their faces, and then he was scooping them up and carrying them, one under each arm like a football, his lungs burning from exertion but they had to go, they had to go *right now* and the tree was cracking and Stetson was yelling and then *whoosh!* the tree fell just behind him, snow spraying everywhere.

He dropped Jennifer and Bonnie and doubled over, his hands on his knees, his lungs gasping, burning, begging for air. They were talking but Luke couldn't hear them over the rush in his ears and the adrenaline spiking in his system.

Finally, his heart rate slowed down just a tad, and he could hear again. Stetson was checking Jennifer over, and she was telling him she was fine, nothing was wrong, and then he'd start all over again. God, he'd turned into a real mother hen since she got pregnant.

Hold on. Bonnie? Where's Bonnie?

He straightened and scanned the area until his eyes fell on her, sitting on a rock above the snow line, staring off to the mountains. He pushed through the snow.

"How ya doing?" His voice came out gruffer than he'd intended but he couldn't take it back now.

"Okay," she said but the shake in her voice belied her answer and he slipped behind her, wrapping an arm awkwardly around her shoulders, even occasionally patting her on the head when he thought of it. She didn't say anything for a long time, and then finally, "Thanks, Luke. And…thanks for saving us. I don't normally get picked up and toted around by a guy on Christmas Eve, so, you know, bonus points for originality."

He could hear the smile in her voice, and he struggled to come up with something to help her completely take her mind off what just happened.

Just then, he saw a tan and black form turn its majestic head to stare at him. A pair of piercing yellow eyes blinked.

"Look," he whispered, pointing at the owl. "It's a great horned owl." She followed his arm to find the stately bird amongst the trees, its browns and tans blending into the scenery so perfectly, it was only its movement that made it possible to spot it.

"Oh…" she breathed softly. "I've never seen one in real life before."

"C'mon, Luke!" Stetson hollered. "We need to figure out how to pull this pine tree back to the truck."

The owl took off, wings flapping silently through

the air, and Bonnie gave a moan of disappointment at its disappearance.

Luke pulled away and headed to Stetson, pretending that he didn't care that Stetson had interrupted their birdwatching adventures. That he hadn't been enjoying the flowery scent that had wafted up from Bonnie's hair and into his nose. That he hadn't been aware of her soft curves pressed against his body.

He heard Sticks thrashing through the underbrush and then a small flock of birds taking to flight as he scared them away. Luke rolled his eyes at his goofy dog. If Sticks thought he could catch a bird, he was in for a world of disappointment.

Together, Stetson and Luke worked to jerry-rig some straps and dragged the tree back to the truck, chests heaving by the time they got there. The cold air was burning in Luke's lungs after they finally got the tree loaded and strapped down. They secured the axes and then Stetson called out, "Hey, we're ready to go!"

Jennifer waded through the snow towards the truck. "Carmelita packed a lunch for us, with a hot thermos of coffee and everything. Why don't we stay out here and eat?"

Luke was taken aback. She wanted to just…sit out here? And do nothing but eat and hang out? That was so…unproductive. Didn't they need to hurry back to the Miller Farm and feed the animals or plan next year's crops or something?

And then he remembered that this whole weekend was supposed to be nothing but relaxing and having fun. It was such an odd thought, he had to force himself not to ask that they let him head back to his farm right then. He had about a half dozen projects in the barn that he could stand to spend some time on, and just hanging out was…pointless.

But dammit, he'd agreed – no, been shanghaied into – this weekend, and he wasn't about to be rude to Jennifer, even if Stetson probably deserved it. She'd think she'd done something to piss him off, and he didn't want to make a pregnant woman get all sniffly and emotional on him.

Or any female at all, come to think of it.

Everyone began digging into the two picnic baskets that Carmelita had filled to the brim and as Luke began to suck down the beef stew, balancing on a rock as he ate, he began to question why it was he hadn't hired a Carmelita of his own. He and ol' Willie swapped cooking duties for dinner, and he wasn't sure which he hated more – eating ol' Willie's burnt food, or the nights where he was the one in charge of cooking. At this point, it was kind of a toss-up.

Sticks found a stick – *finally*, something he could catch – and flopped down in the snow, happily chewing his way through it, content as a bear in a honeypot.

"What's your dog's name?" Bonnie asked.

"Sticks," Luke said.

She burst into laughter.

"Listen, if you haven't thought of a name for him yet, you don't have to pick one right now," she said dryly, once she stopped laughing.

"No, really, that's his name. Three guesses as to why I named him that, and the first two don't count."

"Really?" she asked, surprised. "Sticks? You're an original fellow, aren't you?"

"One of a kind," he drawled and winked at her. She laughed again, and he realized that he really liked hearing that sound.

A lot.

And that scared him.

A lot.

CHAPTER 6

BONNIE

*T*HEY TUMBLED INTO THE HOUSE, laughing and unwrapping their scarves and pulling off their gloves as they went.

"Carmelita, we're home!" Jennifer called. Bonnie's nose twitched.

Is that…gingerbread cookies? Oh God, I've died and gone to heaven!

They wandered through the house, looking for Carmelita, and finally found her in the living room, surrounded by boxes, Christmas music playing softly in the background. She wiped quickly at her face and Bonnie realized that she'd been crying.

"*Mis hijos,* how was your trip?" she asked, quickly standing up and brushing at her skirt. Her perfectly clean skirt.

What is she so upset about? Bonnie's heart hurt at the idea of this sweet woman enduring sadness of any kind.

"Great," Stetson said. "Luke and I are going to bring in the tree, but I wanted to make sure we knew where the stand was for it before we lugged it in."

"Oh yes, I have placed it by the window already. It is ready for your tree." And there it was, directly in front of the large window overlooking the backyard. The window was going to frame the Christmas tree perfectly – a picture-perfect Christmas card in the making.

Stetson and Luke dragged the tree in, with only a minimal amount of mumbled swearing and after a few more choice words, they got the tree stabilized and water into its base. Everyone stood back to admire the tree before they got to work on the ornaments.

It was then that Bonnie realized why Carmelita had been sniffly when they came in. The Christmas decorations coming out of the box were not the standard Target ornaments; they appeared to be handmade antiques.

"Oh Stetson, this is so beautiful," Jennifer breathed, pulling an antique silver ornament out of the box, the arms of the angel twinkling between the tarnished sections.

Carmelita said quietly, "That was one of the ornaments that your great-great-grandparents brought with them across the United States, Stetson."

"Where did you find these?" Stetson asked as Jennifer laid it in his hands, looking down at it in wonder.

"I went up into the attic today while you were getting the tree, and found these boxes. After your mother passed away," she made the sign of the cross, "your father asked me to pack them away. I knew you did not remember them, and I wanted to surprise you. My Christmas gift to you."

He stood from the couch and moved to her side. "Thank you, Carma," he whispered. Bonnie couldn't help it; she felt her eyes prick with tears. The love between them was palpable.

"If only Wyatt and Declan were here to see them, too," she said, stepping away, straightening her skirt and smoothing it again, fiddling, hiding her emotions, staring out the window as if the most fascinating play ever conceived was being put on in the backyard in that very moment.

"Now Carmelita, we both know that isn't possible," Stetson said, exasperation filling his voice. "Wyatt couldn't come even if he wanted to, and even if he could, I wouldn't want him here. He has a lot of growing up to do, and Declan needs to stop defending him."

"I know," she said, her voice laced with pain. "I cannot stop wishing all of my boys to love each other, though." She paused for just a moment and then said, "I will go get polish for the ornaments." She hurried from the room.

A silence sat, smothering and unbreakable, with only Bing Crosby's voice daring to croon in their ears:

Christmas Eve will find me

Where the love light gleams
I'll be home for Christmas
If only in my dreams

Finally, Jennifer gave a strained smile to Bonnie. "Come check out this wonderful treasure. It puts all Walmart decorations to shame." Bonnie hurried over and ooohhh'd and awwww'd over the delicate antique angel, with a yellowed dress and an ever-so-slightly crooked golden halo hovering above its head.

The music changed to a slightly more upbeat song – *Wonderful Christmas Time* – and soon, they were laughing again. Luke draped a twine garland with red bobbles hanging off it around his neck, striking a pose by the tree as he did so. Bonnie laughed until her belly ached and Jennifer polished the silver ornaments and Carmelita brought in trays of gingerbread cookies and coffee and milk and Stetson and Luke argued about who was the tallest and thus had the honor of putting the angel on the top of the tree and the music played, and Bonnie felt a kind of peace and love that she thought only existed in movies. *Cheesy* movies.

But sitting there beneath the twinkling lights of the tree, watching the antics of her friends, she realized that even without her family there, she could still love Christmas. Luke won the battle and after placing the angel on top of the tree, he climbed down from the dining room chair and smiled triumphantly at Bonnie. She couldn't hide the smile that spread across her features and then…his eyes darkened and her breath quickened and she blushed and her gaze dropped to her lap.

She hurried to push the next piece of popcorn onto the needle and down the garland that she was supposed to be making and then she felt the couch shift as Luke sat down. He popped some popcorn into his mouth and said, "Look at me, helping out! Now you don't have to string that popcorn!"

She laughed while rolling her eyes. "Yes, your help is overwhelming me," she said dryly. "I just don't know how to handle it."

"Here, how about this?" he asked, and placed a piece of popcorn at her lips. Her breath hitched and she opened her mouth automatically and he placed the piece inside gently, and then...

Did he just brush his fingertips against my lips?

She bit her bottom lip, staring into his dreamy dark chocolate eyes and she wasn't sure she would ever breathe again, and then...

The rafters shook and the window panes rattled and a wind tore through the pine trees outside like the howling of an angry god.

"What the—!" Stetson exclaimed, putting the ornament down that he was working on and rushing to the window. Everyone followed, staring out into the darkness.

The darkness only broken up by the snowflakes drifting to the ground as far as the eye could see.

CHAPTER 7

LUKE

*H*E'D BEEN STARING at Bonnie's lips, having the most amazing daydream ever, where he was envisioning kissing her and running his fingers through her lush, dark hair, and then…

The damn weather hit. And hit *hard*. He stared out into the semi-darkness, white snowflakes dancing in the wind, whipping into dizzying circles, dropping to the ground only to be sucked back up again, and realized that the weather report calling for only an inch of snow could not possibly be right.

Stetson reached that conclusion the same time Luke did. Their eyes met and he knew Stets was thinking the same thing he was – they had to figure out an emergency plan now, before the electricity cut off and they were all up a shit creek without any preparations for it.

"Darlin'," Stetson said, guiding Jennifer out of the

living room and to the base of the stairs, "we need to gather up blankets, flashlights, pillows, sweaters, matches, candles – whatever you might think we would need if the lights go out. Bonnie, would you go with her?" Bonnie nodded and hurried up the stairs after Jennifer.

Luke pulled his cell phone out of his pocket and called Ol' Willie. He wanted to be sure he was ready to cover the farm. With a blizzard brewing, who knew how long it'd be before Luke could make it back home.

"Hey," Ol' Willie said, cranky as always.

"Hey, we seem to be on the receiving end of a major storm here at Stetson's place. How's it look on the farm?"

"Wind's kicked up and can't see for shit outside – visibility done disappeared. Don't you worry 'bout us. I already done strung a line from the house to the barn, so I can keep them horses fed no matter what. Best you don't come on home – this damn box canyon just makes the snowstorms worse. It's not safe to drive now. You'd land your ass in the borrow pit."

Luke knew he was right, but it was hard to sit on the sidelines. He'd never been away from his farm during a major snowstorm, and was usually the one to string the rope from the corner of the house to the barn so he could move between the buildings even in zero visibility to keep the horses fed no matter what. Knowing that Ol' Willie had thought to do that without being asked made him more appreciative than ever to have hired such a reliable employee.

Especially since his employer had been busy making kissy faces with a girl...

"Well, keep me updated if you can – if the phone lines stay active. I'm gonna help Stetson batten down the hatches."

"Yup," Ol' Willie said, and then the line went dead. Most other people might think that he was angry or pissed about something to end a conversation that way, but Luke wasn't offended. Ol' Willie just wasn't much for wasting time with social niceties like "hello" and "goodbye."

Carmelita came in from the kitchen, worry etched into her face.

"That wind did not sound so good," she said, worrying her lower lip between her teeth. "Was the weatherman wrong about this storm?"

Stetson was looking on his phone. "Looks like it – the Weather Channel is saying that this has been upgraded to a full-blown blizzard. They're estimating anywhere between six inches to two feet of snow by the time it passes."

Luke gulped. Even for Long Valley, that was a lot of snow to fall in one storm.

Another gust of wind buffeted the house and the lights flickered. The achingly cheerful Christmas music continued to play in the background; unable to handle it anymore, Luke turned off the stereo system. Now was *not* the time to sing along to *White Christmas*.

"Stetson, I need my heart medicine," Carmelita said, her hand on his arm, staring up into his face. "Maybe you should take me to my house now. I need to find my flashlight and blankets before the power dies."

"No, you should stay here with us," Jennifer said, entering the room with her arms heaping with blankets. Luke wondered how she could even see over the stack. Bonnie trailed behind her with an equally large stack of pillows in her arms. "Stetson can go get your heart medicine and bring it back here. Then we only need to worry about keeping one home warm and safe."

Carmelita hesitated for a moment and then nodded, acquiescing to the wisdom of this plan, but said emphatically, "I must go with you. It is too hard to explain everything that I need." She hurried to wrap up in her coat and scarf as the winds continued to howl around the farmhouse, whistling through the trees, shaking the window panes as it roared past.

Sticks, content up to that point to a chew on a bone in the corner – Carmelita had refused to let him bring a stick inside – suddenly made his presence known when he began whining. He started trying to wedge himself underneath the couch, the far end bouncing up and down as Sticks wiggled his way to the back until only his tail was sticking out.

Wimp. Luke couldn't help loving his goofy-ass dog, even if he was damn worthless for just about anything but chewing up sticks.

Everyone just stared at the couch, one end of it hovering about six inches off the ground, and then Bonnie said dryly, "Well, no sitting on the couch for a while."

The smiles appeared for just a moment, and then disappeared as everyone sprung into action. Luke set to work filling up pots with water, since the well didn't work without electricity to pump the water out of the ground. Jennifer and Bonnie went back to work to find candles and flashlights and matches. Sticks continued whining, because that's what he was best at, and Stetson and Carmelita took off for her small white cottage.

It was about 25 feet off from the house, although Luke was all too aware that 25 feet might as well be a universe away when you couldn't see. He was sure Stetson would take good care of Carma, though, and get them both back to the house safely.

After Luke filled every pot and bowl he could find, he headed for the back porch, where the firewood was stacked against the outside wall. He'd refill the firewood nook under the stairs in the living room. Stetson's natural gas heater relied on electricity to keep the pilot light lit and to run the fan that blew the hot air around, so as soon as the electricity went out – which was a *when*, not an *if* at this point – so did the heat.

He was about two-thirds of the way done when everything went dark.

Dammit.

He kept hauling the firewood in, in the semi-darkness of the house, wanting to get as much firewood inside as possible to minimize the number of times they'd need to open up the backdoor and let the heat escape out of the house.

Once he had the firewood nook filled to the brim, he started stacking it in the fireplace. A fire would serve as a three-fold bonus at this point: Heat, light, *and* security. There was something peaceful about the crackling of a fire that would soothe everyone's nerves.

Once he'd filled the fireplace with some smaller pieces and set some large logs on the hearth off to the side, to feed into the fire once it was established, he set to work on getting it going. He'd done all he could at this point to ready the house; it was time for him to make sure everyone stayed nice and warm.

He got a small fire going in no time, and started feeding the larger logs into it. Hopefully Bonnie and Jennifer would show up with some candles and they could light them and place them around the living room. Although the fireplace gave off light, it would still just feel better to ward off the darkness.

He heard coughing behind him and turned to see Bonnie and Jennifer, dust-streaked faces scrunched up as they continued to sneeze up a storm, bundles in their arms.

"What…what happened to you two?" he asked, and then began laughing as Bonnie attempted to push her hair out of her face with the back of her hand

and only ended up with more streaks of dirt on her face.

"Well, I started to think after Carmelita brought all of those ornaments down from the attic that I bet that there was other stuff up there that we could use tonight," Jennifer said as she set the bundles down. "So we went looking, and found sleeping bags." She grinned triumphantly at Luke. "I figured Stetson probably hadn't been camping since his dad died, maybe even before that, so any camping equipment would be up there, not in the garage. I know how Carmelita's brain works."

Bonnie sneezed twice more in succession and then grinned at Luke. "And apparently, I'm just incapable of saying no." He chuckled – he couldn't help himself. She had a better sense of humor than any girl he'd ever met before, especially for a girl who currently had a spider's web strung across her scalp.

"So inquiring minds want to know – how did Carmelita manage to bring down all of these ornaments from the attic without ending up…looking like you two?" he asked with a grin, gesturing at their dirty faces and even dirtier hair.

"We discussed that and decided that it can only be explained away by saying that Carmelita is magic."

"She has magical powers where dust does not dare to land upon her," Bonnie added with a grin.

"Well, whatever her magical capabilities are, she's not gonna be happy to see two homeless urchins have taken up residence in her living room," Luke pointed out. "There's pots of water in the kitchen – I'd clean up before her and Stets come back. Oh, and did you guys find any candles?"

"Not yet," Jennifer called back, her flashlight on her phone leading the way to the kitchen. "I'd meant to look through the pantry here in the kitchen for that, but got sidetracked."

Luke followed them into the kitchen, envious of their laughter as they attempted to clean each other. How long had it been since he'd allowed himself to just let go and let out a belly laugh? To chill out and not fret about things to come? To just totally and completely relax?

He'd started to tonight, as they'd decorated the tree. When Bonnie was stringing the popcorn and he'd been busy feeding her, he'd felt a lightness inside that seemed almost alien to him. He'd gone back into work mode once the storm really kicked up, though, focused on the task at hand.

But somehow, Bonnie and Jennifer were able to be focused and still have fun. That was *their* magic trick. A magic trick he wanted to learn.

Taking his phone out of his pocket, he put it into airplane mode. No sense trying to waste battery searching for a signal in this storm. He flicked on the flashlight app and began hunting through the pantry. Organized as it was, it only took him seconds to find the candles and matches, conveniently stored next to each other. He picked up the basket of candles, balancing the matchbooks on top, and headed back to the living room. Time to give their new home a romantic feel.

Complete with rafter-shuddering gusts of wind.

After lighting and placing the candles around the living room, he decided he ought to convince Sticks to come out from underneath the couch.

"C'mon, buddy," he said, down on his hands and knees, looking underneath the couch. Two bright eyes stared back at him, not moving. "You can't hide underneath here all night. We need to sit on this couch." He made kissy noises and snapped his fingers a few times. Sticks whined but didn't move. "C'mon boy, get out of there."

Preferably before someone walks in here and sees me down on the ground like this with my ass sticking up in the air.

"No luck?" Bonnie said behind him.

Dammit.

He sat back on his haunches. "Not yet," he admitted.

"Let me have a go at it." She got down on her hands and knees too, sticking her ever-so-fine ass up in the air, capturing Luke's attention. Forget Sticks – he was happy to just stare at Bonnie's curvy ass.

"C'mon boy, come here," she said softly, patting the floor in front of her.

He sensed movement and realized that Sticks was almost out from underneath the couch. With a wiggle of his hip bones, he finally popped out and trotted the few steps to Bonnie, licking her face, tail wagging a million miles a minute.

Luke opened up his mouth to protest – *just a minute here, that's* my *dog!* – when he realized he'd sound like a jealous idiot if he actually let those words escape his mouth. He swallowed hard instead as he listened to Bonnie's half-hearted protests and laughter at Sticks' overly enthusiastic tonguing.

"I just bathed, mister," she told him sternly, and Luke was happy to note that at least in this regard, Sticks listened to Bonnie as well as he listened to Luke, which was exactly not at all.

She looked up at Luke and grinned. "You've got a real sweetheart of a dog here," she said, as Sticks' tail thumped against the couch. Another gust of wind rattled the rafters of the house and Luke expected Sticks to dive under the couch again, but instead, he seemed perfectly content to hang out with his new best friend, even curling up on her lap like a ridiculously oversized lapdog.

Instead of dumping him off onto the floor, she ran her hand along Sticks' body. "Hey, buddy," she crooned. "You're such a good dog. Not very brave but awfully sweet." Sticks thumped his tail at her tone of voice and Luke couldn't bite back his laughter any longer.

"Sticks, you dumbass, she's insulting you." Sticks looked up at him, a doggy grin on his face, his tail still thumping the couch. Luke reached out to rub him across his knuckle-headed skull when his hand collided with Bonnie and she looked up at him, her face lit only by the dancing flames of the fireplace and candles. She was biting her lip again and he stroked his fingers across her hand, ever so gently, and she shivered—

"Anyone want more gingerbread cookies?" Jennifer came into the room with a tray overloaded with goodies.

Luke yanked his hand back guiltily and Bonnie turned red – even in the firelight, he could see it – and Jennifer bustled around, rearranging the candles to distribute the light in the room to better effect, oblivious to Bonnie and Luke and the blush covering her friend's face.

Luke scrambled to find something to say. *Anything* to cover the awkward silence he felt sure astronauts were currently picking up on radar from space, it was so damn obvious.

"I wonder if I should go out and look for Stetson and Carmelita," he said, rising to his feet. "They've been gone for a long time." He crossed to the window to peer out into the storm. The swirls of snow hadn't died down; if anything, they'd only gotten stronger since he'd looked outside last. A movement caught his eye and he saw, struggling through the snow, two faint figures, stumbling.

Stetson and Carmelita. And they were heading the wrong way.

CHAPTER 8

LUKE

"*O*H SHIT!" he exclaimed, and ran to the backdoor, grabbing his jacket from the hook hanging there and throwing it on before heading outside. He didn't take the time to bundle up further – he *had* no time to bundle up further.

He struck out through the snow, his feet sinking into the newly fallen snow on top and then hitting the harder, older snow underneath before finally finding solid ground. Each step was laborious, pushing his thigh muscles to the max. His cowboy boots were not exactly the best foot gear to be wearing in a snowstorm but now wasn't the time to worry about that, either.

He looked up occasionally as he pushed through the snow, making sure he was still heading the right direction, and would occasionally change course as needed. It was probably only minutes but it felt like years before he finally reached the pair, grabbing the large, heavy suitcase from Stetson's frozen fingers – *what the hell is in here?* – and then draped his arm around Carmelita's shoulders, shouting to them above the wind that they needed to follow him.

He began guiding them back towards the farmhouse, trying to hurry Carmelita through the snow while also protecting her against the worst of the blasts of frozen air.

Then she stumbled and curled up on the ground and didn't seem to understand that she had to get back up and that's when he realized that he had no more time left to help her walk. She was far past that. He shoved the suitcase back into Stetson's arms, Stetson's frozen limbs making it hard to grab the case but Luke didn't care. He didn't have time to care.

He scooped Carma up into his arms and began pushing through the snow as fast as he could. His jeans were frozen and wet, sending pricks of pain through his legs with every step. He couldn't stay out here much longer, either, or he wouldn't be much use to Stetson or Carmelita.

Finally, oh thank God *finally*, he made it to the back porch and just as he was trying to figure out how to open the door without dropping Carma, Bonnie opened it.

He carried Carma inside, through the kitchen and into the living room, setting her down on the couch beside the fireplace, pulling at her jacket and scarf, trying to get the wet sodden overclothes away from her skin. Jennifer reappeared in the living room with a stack of towels and the three of them set to work warming up Stetson and Carmelita. Stetson was shaking so bad, Luke wondered if he'd fall off the couch in the grip of his shivers, but it was Carmelita who scared him more. Her lips were blue and she was staring over his shoulder, not seeming to realize he was there.

He briskly rubbed her head and neck with a hand towel while Bonnie did the same to her hands and feet. He was destroying the bun that she always had her hair pinned up in, but he didn't care. She could re-pin it later.

His legs were painfully cold and wet in his jeans and cowboy boots and he knew he needed to change clothes if he was ever going to warm up but he also knew that Stetson and Carma were in much worse shape than he was. He had no time to change, not right now.

Jennifer's worried questions and murmurs of love were repeating again and again in the quiet room. "Oh Stetson, what happened? What took you so long? I can't believe this happened. I'm worried about you. Talk to me. Tell me you're okay. What happened?" Her plaintive voice tore at Luke and he realized, perhaps for the first time, how much she *truly* loved Stetson. Sure, he'd thought she loved Stetson and they seemed to make each other happy, but this…

This was more than that. This was someone in the deepest of pain, crying out.

"Took…longer…than…I   thought," Stetson

rasped out. The room was dead silent, only the crackling of the fireplace and Stetson's rough voice to break up the silence. "Kept thinking...of things to bring." Luke remembered the weight of the bag and wondered if Carma had decided to pack most of her house up in it. They must not have realized how quickly the storm was gathering strength. "Then came back...back outside...and the snow was in our tracks...couldn't see them. All gone...couldn't see house...all gone...Everything white."

Jennifer took a large towel and began briskly rubbing his head and ears. "Shhh...shhh....you can tell me everything later," she crooned. "Let's warm you up."

Carmelita's eyes began to focus again. Her teeth were chattering so hard, she wouldn't have been able to speak even if she wanted to, but Luke was heartened by the progress. When a body doesn't shiver at all, that was when they were close to death. Teeth chattering was a welcome indication of life returning.

"Hey beautiful," Bonnie said, stroking Carmelita's hair away from her scalp. "How're ya doing?"

Carmelita gave a nod of the head and Luke guessed that was all she could manage at the moment.

He and Bonnie's eyes met over the top of Carmelita, and he realized in that moment how much he wanted to kiss her, to hold her tight. Seeing how fragile they all were, how close the human body could come to death in just minutes, it made him want to hold Bonnie close and never let her go.

And the way her breath quickened and she began biting her lip and her eyes seemed to darken, he knew she was thinking the same thing.

And it only sorta, kinda terrified him.

CHAPTER 9

BONNIE

STETSON AND CARMELITA slowly became more coherent and along with it, Carma's lips began to turn a light pink color, a sign of progress that made Bonnie want to cry with happiness. It had been so damn scary to see her literally frozen, a statue of ice and blue and stone. First Stetson and then Carma went and changed into dry clothes, trying to hurry the warming process along.

Luke excused himself to change also, and it was only then that Bonnie realized how frozen he must've been. When he stood up, she discovered that there was a large puddle at his feet from the melted snow. He hadn't said a word of complaint the whole time he tended to Carmelita.

Jennifer hurried to retrieve more towels, these looking...distinctly less pristine than the first batch she'd brought in. "Stetson only has so many nice sets of towels," she said with a laugh at Bonnie's questioning look. "When the electricity comes back on, Carmelita's going to have quite a batch of laundry to do."

"Somehow, I don't think she'll mind," Bonnie said with a smile and for just a moment, the two friends stared at each other. Then it hit Jennifer and she pulled Bonnie in for a hug and began crying on her shoulder.

"He was so stiff and cold and he wasn't talking and…I thought he was gone, Bonnie!" She hiccuped as the tears ran down her cheeks. "It was so damn scary to see him like that. Oh Bonnie, what if Luke hadn't noticed? Just a few minutes more, and I don't know…" She broke off, unable to continue. But Bonnie knew what she meant. Life was so damn precarious.

Jennifer pulled back from their embrace. "I…I should get some hot water going. Carma will want some tea when she comes back." She hurried from the living room, dabbing her eyes as she went, leaving only Bonnie and Sticks. Bonnie mopped up the puddle from Luke's clothes and then sat down on the floor next to Sticks with a sigh.

"Well, boy," she said, scratching him behind the ears, "today was an adventure that I'm not sure I ever want to repeat."

"I think I can agree to that."

Bonnie whirled around, surprised at Luke's voice behind her. She hadn't heard him come back down the stairs. He had his flashlight on his phone turned off, which left them in the dim light of the living room, only the flickering of the fireplace and the candles to break through the darkness.

He crossed over and knelt beside her, and began giving belly rubs to Sticks. His tongue lolled out happily and Bonnie could only laugh at the sight. "I *think* your dog may be happy," she said wryly.

"Yeah, just a little." Luke smiled at her and her heart skipped a beat. In the light of the dancing flames, his cheekbones were thrown into high relief, and his eyes...they were dancing in the darkness, too.

"So where is your family? Why aren't you with them for Christmas?" Bonnie finally asked, if only to have *something* to say, since breathing normally seemed to have become optional and she needed to have something to distract herself. He was quite possibly the most handsome man she'd ever laid eyes on, and her breathing seemed to become...erratic every time he got close to her.

As soon as she asked the question, though, his mouth tightened and he looked away and she knew she'd hit a sore spot. She opened her mouth to apologize when he began to speak, and so she closed her mouth with a snap. She wouldn't be so rude as to interrupt him *after* asking him an unwanted question.

"My dad's here in the valley. We see each other sometimes, just in passing. At Frank's Feed & Fuel or the grocery store or whatever. He's not...we're not close.

"And my siblings...there's a pair of twins who are

younger than me – five years younger. A girl and a boy, so no, they're not identical.

"They both left as soon as they graduated from high school. Literally. They left that night when graduation ended and I've only seen them a couple of times since. They hate Sawyer and make no bones about it.

"And my mom…well, she and I haven't seen each other since the Christmas of 2002."

Bonnie sucked in a quick breath. *How was that even possible? How could someone go that long without seeing their mother?* She tried to imagine for a moment not seeing her mom for years and years, but quickly gave up. Her mom was one of her best friends.

Luke began telling a story, settling in beside her on the floor, his hand coasting gently over Stick's fur again and again, in a trance of remembrance.

"My mom had hated Sawyer – *all* of Long Valley – for a long time. After I was born, I think she had postpartum depression because she just sank inside herself. At least, that's what I heard later. Obviously, I don't remember it myself." He shot Bonnie a smile without humor and then turned his gaze back to Sticks, who was floating on a cloud of pure joy as Luke continued to pet him.

"Things got real rough between my parents – she blamed him for taking her away from everything and everyone she loved. She'd gotten pregnant with me, you see. I was the reason they got married. She never missed an opportunity to make me regret this failing of mine – that I'd forced her to marry a man that I'm not sure she ever really loved."

He took a deep breath and turned his gaze to the dancing flames in the fireplace. "She was on the verge of leaving Dad again, when she found out she was pregnant. And with twins, to boot! She didn't know how to care for three children by herself, so she reluctantly stayed, but it was rough. It was always rough. My parents were like oil and water, and are the reason that marriage and I...we're just never gonna happen. After seeing what a bad one can do to you... well, I just won't do it. Not for me.

"In 2002, winter came early and just stayed. Usually up here in the mountains, we'll get an early snowstorm and then things warm up, and that repeats a few times before the snow really sticks for the winter. Not that year. It came and it stayed, and my mom slowly started going stir crazy. I was almost 13 and not the most observant or understanding teenage boy on the face of the planet, so I didn't get what was happening to her.

"On Christmas Eve, my mom became bound and determined to go get milk. Sure, we were out, but we could've survived without it. We would've been fine. But there she was, out in the driveway, spinning donuts on the ice, plowing into the snowbank, getting stuck...she was a mess. Dad and I went out to help her, and finally got her heading the right direction. She disappeared down the driveway, her red taillights blazing in the night, and then..."

He stopped for just a moment. Nothing but the crackling of the fireplace broke the silence that settled over the world.

"I've never seen her again."

He turned and looked Bonnie in the eye and she saw the pain, the anger, the confusion, painted on his face. Her heart broke for him, and she put out her hand to stroke his face, her fingers running over the rough stubble on his jaw, and then, her comfort changed to lust in the dancing firelight. His eyes grew hooded with desire and her heart began trying to beat its way out of her chest and slowly, ever so damn slowly, he moved towards her, his eyes questioning – *Are you sure?* – and her heart answering – *Yes, oh please, yes.*

His mouth moved over hers, gently at first, and then with more passion as his tongue ran along the seam of her lips. She opened her mouth and let him in and he shoved his hand into her hair, burying it, angling her mouth under his and her heart thrummed in her chest, maybe right out of her chest, and she couldn't breathe – oh God, she couldn't breathe—

A soft clearing of the throat came then, and then a little louder, finally registering in her mind and they sprung apart, guilty as two teenagers caught making out under the bleachers by their teacher.

Jennifer was trying – and failing miserably – at hiding her grin. "I think some other people were planning on coming into the living room soon," she said tactfully. Bonnie's cheeks were painted a brilliant red and she quickly scooted up and sat on the couch, curling up on the end, smiling maniacally at Jennifer.

"Of course!" she said too loudly, too enthusiastically. Jennifer laughed then, and Luke muttered something about checking in on...and his voice trailed off too quietly to hear *exactly* what it was that he was checking on, before he hurried out of the room like his ass was on fire.

"So, remind me again – what was it that you were saying about Luke not being your kind of guy?" Jennifer said with a sassy grin as she sat next to Bonnie.

"Well, he wasn't," Bonnie mumbled. "He was my Voyeur Cowboy then."

"'Voyeur Cowboy'?" Jennifer repeated with a laugh. "That's an *awesome* nickname. Have you told Luke that you'd christened him that?"

Bonnie blanched. "No, somehow I left that out of the discussion."

Just then, Carmelita came into the room, wrapped up in a sweater, looking a little tired but otherwise none worse for the wear.

"Oh!" Jennifer said at her arrival, and jumped to her feet. "I filled the kettle with water but then got sidetracked by Stetson! I thought we could put the kettle over the flames and warm it up to make some tea."

"What a lovely idea," Carma said with a tired smile. Jennifer hurried and returned from the kitchen, kettle in hand, and they set to work trying to figure out how to heat the water over the open flame.

"Gosh, I'm glad we don't have to do this every time we want some warm water!" Jennifer said as they finally settled the kettle into the coals. "I don't think I could make it as a pioneer. I'm too spoiled."

Stetson came walking in, all wrapped up in his own sweater and wool socks and said, "But just think how cute you'd be in a bonnet!"

She stuck her tongue out at him and he only laughed.

They settled in beside the fire and Luke finally reappeared, apparently having finally finished his very urgent mission. Somehow, as soon as he walked in, everyone else rearranged themselves and the only open place to sit was right next to Bonnie.

She was going to give them points for effectiveness, but not for subtlety. She'd seen billboards with more subtlety.

Jennifer gathered a tea tray from the kitchen – she seemed so happy to be serving Carmelita for once. Carma protested at one point, but was overruled. It was about time someone took care of her. Jennifer also dug out an old tape player that actually ran on batteries, and put in a tape of old Christmas carols. Bonnie grinned as *Silver Bells* came warbling out of the speakers, the sound quality just atrocious.

It was perfectly imperfect.

They chatted and laughed and the winds blew

and the rafters shuddered and yet, somehow, Bonnie had never felt so safe and warm as she did right then.

She'd thought she would be homesick this Christmas, the first one she'd ever spent away from her family, but she realized as the evening slowly drifted on, that family and love was wherever she wanted it to be.

But as the evening drifted towards night, Carmelita's blinks slowly became longer and Bonnie nudged Luke, jerking her head towards Carma. He gave her a quizzical look for just a moment and then his eyes went wide with understanding.

"I'm pretty tired," he said loudly, with a large stretch. "Maybe we should put out those sleeping bags."

Carmelita's eyes sprang fully open and she eyed the dusty bags in question dubiously. Bonnie realized that Carma probably wouldn't be super excited about sleeping on the floor. "If we roll out four sleeping bags, then that'd leave enough room for Carmelita to sleep on the couch," she volunteered.

They quickly got to work rolling the sleeping bags out, and getting Carmelita settled in on the couch. The fire had died down to just embers, so Stetson stoked the fire, wanting to keep it producing heat for as long as possible. Luke offered to set an alarm on his phone for three in the morning so he could stoke it again, something that Bonnie was both simultaneously impressed that he'd thought of, and happy she didn't have to do.

Bonnie blew out the candles while Jennifer closed the doors leading into the living room, trapping the heat from the fireplace into the room. Because it was an older farmhouse, each doorway had a door and wasn't just an open archway. Bonnie was quickly seeing the reasoning behind being able to block off certain rooms in the house as needed. Sure, this home wouldn't qualify as an "open floor plan" home that all of the real estate agents loved to tout in their ads, but then again, some things were only practical if you had forced air heat.

Which, at the moment, they most assuredly did not have.

The room slowly grew quieter as the whispers of Stetson and Jennifer died off, and Carmelita's heavy breathing started to fill the air. Bonnie shifted in her sleeping bag, curling up on her side – who thought that sleeping on the floor was a good idea? – when she came face to face with Luke, his eyes trained right on her. They stared at each other and he didn't blink and she couldn't breathe and—

"*What?*" she finally whispered when she couldn't stand it anymore.

"Just trying to figure out if your hair is brown or red."

A startled laugh spilled out of her. "What?!" she hissed, trying to keep her voice low so she didn't wake up the others.

He reached his hand out from underneath his sleeping bag and lightly touched her hair.

"During the day, it looks dark and I just thought it was brown, but now…in the firelight, it looks sorta red."

His hand ran softly through her hair, stroking it away from her face, and she shivered, his touch sending electrical sparks through her.

She wanted to say something sassy and fun, like, "Do you pick up all the chicks with lines like that?" but then he ran his thumb over her lower lip, which is when her control completely left her. She opened her mouth just slightly and flicked her tongue against the pad of his thumb. His breath caught and she knew – just knew – that he was having just as hard a time breathing and thinking as she was.

And she couldn't lie – she wasn't sure if that made her happy or terrified her.

Because he was a *cowboy*. Everything about him, from the tips of his boots to the crown of his cowboy hat to his plaid shirts in between – today it was a blue plaid as opposed to his red plaid from yesterday – screamed *cowboy*.

And she was a city girl.

And just what the hell was she supposed to do with that?

CHAPTER 10

LUKE

*A*s soon as Stetson had suggested that they all sleep in the living room to make it easier to keep them warm, Luke had known he'd be in trouble. Stetson was asking him to spend the night lying next to Bonnie, one of the most beautiful women he'd ever laid eyes on.

Who wore sexy red lace underwear – a sight burned into his brain for the rest of his life – and patiently talked a dog out from underneath the couch and doted on Carmelita like she was her own grandmother and listened when he rambled on about The Christmas and was so damn beautiful, it hurt just to look at her.

Not, of course, that this kept him from looking at her. In fact, he didn't seem to be able to stop, even when he should.

She'd lain down and faced the other direction

when they'd first gotten into their sleeping bags, but somehow, she seemed to sense his gaze on the back of her head as they lay there, and eventually, as the others began to sink into sleep, she'd turned over and caught him staring.

And hell, if he was going to be caught, he might as well keep doing it, right? Why force himself to look away, when the colors in her hair were so fascinating? There were just so many different shades in there.

And then, she'd flicked her tongue against the pad of his thumb and he'd sucked in his breath so hard and so fast, he wasn't sure he'd ever need to breathe again…

He pulled his hand away and forced himself to close his eyes.

Tightly.

And count to three.

Because he could not, could *not*, foresee a way of having this evening end the way his dick was currently begging him to end it. Not with Stetson and Jennifer and Carmelita right there, for God's sakes.

He shifted in his sleeping bag, trying to find a comfortable spot to lie. Suddenly, it seemed damned uncomfortable there on the floor.

Or maybe it was just that certain parts of his anatomy weren't very happy.

He rolled back towards her and opened up his eyes. Was she still awake?

Yes, yes she was, and now she was the one staring at him.

"So why aren't you with your family?" he whispered. Because it was something to ask her and because it would get his mind off his dick.

Okay, not really, because that was impossible right now, but perhaps he could just sidetrack it a bit.

"I love Christmas," she whispered back.

He stared at her, waiting to hear what her explanation was for that seemingly random comment.

She shrugged.

"I love everything about Christmas. The music, the presents, the lights, how happy everyone is, the smell of pine trees – even if I never got a real pine tree for my house, I still love going by Christmas tree lots – the snow…it all just says *magic* to me. Maybe I'm just slower to grow up than others, I don't know. But I do know this is my favorite season, my favorite holiday…"

She drew in a deep breath and whispered, "My mom decided that this was the year that she would take my dad and my siblings and my nieces and nephews to Hawaii for Christmas. It was *finally* going to be the winter where she got to spend it away from the cold and the sleet and the snow. I did *not* get my love of snow from my mother," she whispered with a grin.

He grinned back, but inside? He was in shock. Somehow, he'd just assumed that all city girls were like his mom – hating pine trees and mountains and snow. Hating living in the middle of nowhere.

Well, maybe she still doesn't like small towns.

He ignored that cautioning voice for the moment. For just a minute or two, he could pretend that Bonnie was all that he wanted in a woman.

If just for a minute or two.

"So I told my mom that I didn't want to go because I love Christmas, and palm trees and piña coladas on the beach just were not Christmassy enough for me."

She caught her lower lip for just a moment, hesitating, and he knew she was debating how much to tell him. As the fire crackled in the darkness, he held his breath. Would she tell him the truth? Or placate him with a half-truth?

She finally whispered, "But honestly? I couldn't afford the trip."

There. That was something she'd been hiding from everyone else in the world, he'd bet his favorite pair of cowboy boots on it, and yet, here she was, telling it to him.

"I have a stupid amount of student loans, you see, and I've just started making headway on them. It'll be years before I have them paid off. My parents just see that I work at this prestigious accounting firm and think that I'm making the big bucks, but I'm not. Not really. Not after I pay for rent and utilities and my student loans and just life, you know?

"But my parents are so damn proud of me and I don't want to admit the truth to them. I don't want them to know that I'm really not as successful as they think I am."

She smiled, a small, painful smile that held no real happiness in it but she was trying to pretend that it did and she did and she was happy and everything was fine...

But it was written all over her face that she most definitely was *not* fine.

In fact, she seemed a little more miserable than just being a little poor would seem to justify.

"Do you like your job at the prestigious accounting firm?" Luke asked, making a stab at why her face and her smile were so forcibly happy. Why she was trying to pretend as if everything was just fine with her world.

She paused for a second and then shook her head.

"No. I hate it. Like, really, *really* hate it. I'd gone into accounting because I wanted to work with small business owners – help them keep a handle on their finances, fill out their taxes to their best advantage... all of these things that I thought I could do to make a difference in their lives.

"Did you know that small businesses have a failure rate of 50% in the first five years? It's almost always due to money mismanagement. No one starts a restaurant or an office supply store or becomes a plumber because they want to push paper all day. They start these businesses because they have a passion and want to make it come to life, but pushing paper is part of making that passion happen.

"So bills start to overwhelm and they don't know

how to manage cash flow, and pretty soon, they're in over their heads.

"I wanted to be that difference in their lives.

"Instead, I'm in my own paper-pushing hell." She closed her eyes, scrunching them against the pain, against the world, against the reality of it all, and he reached out and stroked her face.

He'd never hated his job – he'd always loved farming and so buying his own farm at age 22 was a dream come true for him. He couldn't imagine dreading going to work every day, and knowing that he'd gotten into a hell of a lot of debt in order to have that job. That sounded…miserable.

He didn't know what to say, or how to comfort her, so he just softly stroked her hair and her face relaxed, smoothing into happy lines.

And then…full relaxation.

And a little snore.

His hand slowed, and then stopped. Her snore got a little louder. She was competing with Stetson now, and he was on the other side of the room.

And how, dear God above, did she fall asleep so quickly? He squinted at her in the semi-darkness.

Bonnie really seemed to be asleep.

He waved his hand in front of her face. She let out another snore. He grinned to himself, debating whether this was something he ought to tease her about right away, or later.

Choices, choices, choices.

He settled back down and closed his eyes, and somehow, between the popping of the fire and the snores of Stetson and Bonnie, and the heavy breathing of Carmelita, and the even louder snores and grunts of Sticks, Luke also fell asleep.

CHAPTER 11

BONNIE

S HE WOKE WITH a big yawn and stretch, trying to work the soreness out of her muscles. Why was she so sore? And, she blinked, trying to focus her eyes, why was she in Jennifer's living room?

It all came back to her – the storm, the electricity, the late-night talk – when Sticks took her movement as an invitation to give her cheek an early morning bath. He panted over her, a happy doggy grin plastered across his face, his doggy breath washing over her in waves.

She coughed, waving her hand in front of her face, trying to push the…questionable-smelling air away, when Luke said groggily, "Sorry. I keep meaning to brush his teeth."

He sat up, pushing a thatch of hair away from his forehead with a yawn. He looked deliciously sleepy and she began regretting separate sleeping bags.

When he stretched, his muscles popping along his arms and shoulders − only a scant wife beater t-shirt to cover his torso − she began to really, really regret separate sleeping bags.

Sticks nudged her, apparently not happy with the amount of attention that she was giving him, and so she gave in and pet him while watching Luke slither out of his sleeping bag and pad over to the fireplace to stoke the fire again. It was cold outside of her sleeping bag and so she snuggled back down inside of it, quite content to curl up and enjoy the warmth.

Sticks flopped down next to her, the weight of him pushing her sideways in the bag as he tried to curl up on as much of the sleeping bag as possible.

"Sticks!" she grunted. "I can't breathe!" Sticks thumped his tail happily on the floor, his tongue lolling out of his mouth. He looked as content as could be.

Luke looked over and grinned. "Yup, he's still listening to you as well as he listens to me," he whispered while laughing.

Deciding that she wasn't going to get any more sleeping done with Sticks around, she forced herself into the upright position, shoving her wayward hair out of her face. Jennifer was still sleeping peacefully, as was Carmelita, but Stetson seemed to have disappeared.

"Where's Stetson?" she whispered.

"Not sure." Luke shrugged and stood up from the fireplace, the fire now roaring and popping behind him. He padded over to the windows to look out.

"Oh Bonnie!" he exclaimed in a strangled gasp. She could tell he was trying to keep his voice low but wasn't succeeding.

She pushed the rest of the way out of her sleeping bag and, snagging a throw blanket on the way to ward off the cold, she tiptoed her way across the room. Sticks lumbered after her, nails clicking on the wood floors as he went.

She stopped short next to Luke, the view before her taking her breath away. It was…gorgeous.

Rolling away from the door and down the small slope to the pine forest that bordered Stetson's backyard, was nothing but a field of white. Small crests of snow broke up the seemingly endlessness of the snow, until the dark browns and greens of the forest paraded against the background.

And more snow was still falling, quiet, large flakes drifting endlessly from the sky. It wasn't the whiteout conditions of the blizzard of yesterday, but rather the kind of peaceful snowfall that was depicted on the front of every Hallmark Christmas card.

"It's gorgeous," she whispered.

"You…don't hate it? Or feel trapped by it?"

"Oh gosh no," she gushed. "I may've been lying to my parents about *all* of the reasons that I wasn't going to join them in Hawaii, but there's a reason why they believed me when I said Hawaii just wasn't Christmassy enough for me. I've always been the Christmas child in the family – the first to want to put up the Christmas tree, the first to want to listen to Christmas music, the one who insists that we should celebrate the Twelve Days of Christmas just so we can spread it out a little more. Snow, pine trees…this is Christmas to me just as much as the presents and music are."

He stared down at her, his expression unreadable, and she wondered if she'd sounded like a true idiot there. She'd dated an ass – his name on his birth certificate was Ryan Petersen although really, "Ass" was a lot more accurate – seriously for about six months and at the end, when they were breaking up, he told her that the *real* reason they weren't working out wasn't because he had an awful temper, but because she was a child who just didn't understand how the world worked.

Which was probably true, but it still hurt to hear. She was a true optimist, and if someone was going to hate that about her, well, there wasn't much she could do to help them.

Which made her optimistic nature quite sad.

Stetson came in the backdoor then, brushing his feet against the mat as he entered, trying to keep the snow out of the house. She could see him through the doorway into the kitchen, a door he must've forgotten to close when he'd gone outside.

Dammit, and Luke looked like he was finally going to say something – tell me what's going through that head of his.

Bonnie bit her tongue in frustration and smiled at Stetson instead.

"Hey, you guys," Stetson said, surprised. "Have you been awake long?"

Bonnie shrugged. "Not long," she whispered back. "But Jennifer and Carmelita are still asleep."

Jennifer made some noise behind them. "Not anymore," she said around her yawn. Her pink John Deere t-shirt hugged her gently rounding stomach, still a surprise to Bonnie every time she saw it. It was like seeing a pastoral painting of the English countryside...with zebras grazing in the pasture instead of sheep. Everything looks normal except that one glaring difference.

But pregnancy looked good on Jennifer. *Everything* looked good on Jennifer – it was a good thing Bonnie loved her or she'd have to hate her on principal just because – but the pregnancy brought out a special glow in her that Bonnie loved to see. Jennifer was going to be one hell of a mother.

Jennifer struggled out of her sleeping bag and made her way over to her husband, snuggling up against him, apparently immune to the cold of the melting snow on his coveralls. "Good morning, darlin'," she breathed, going up on her tippy toes to kiss him.

Bonnie glanced away, not wanting to spy on them during such an intimate moment, and caught Luke's eye instead. He looked...

Well, he looked like he wanted to do exactly what

Jennifer and Stetson were doing. Bonnie nibbled her lower lip, trying to control her impulse to give him exactly what he wanted. His eyes were hooded and locked on her lips. She swallowed hard because her self-control was wavering something fierce and—

"Good morning, *mis hijos*," Carmelita said behind them. Bonnie whirled around to see the older woman smoothing away the wrinkles in her PJs.

"Good morning, Carma!" Bonnie said, ignoring her disappointment at having a potential kiss with Luke interrupted, instead giving Carma a hug and a kiss. It was so nice to see her up and around after her scare yesterday.

"It is still snowing?" she asked, peering around the group to the backyard. Jennifer and Stetson had moved into the living room, closing the door behind them. Bonnie would've sworn that raised the temperature in the living room by a couple of degrees almost instantly.

"Yeah," Stetson said ruefully. "I'd give almost anything to have an updated weather forecast because I have no idea how long this is going to last, but I already tried my cell phone this morning and I have no data access or phone access. The landline is down, too. There's no getting in or out, at least not for a while.

"But the animals are fed and watered for this morning, and we have enough hay stocked up to last the whole winter, so the animals are going to be fine. Heaven forbid we're stuck here for a whole winter," he said with a chuckle that didn't seem to actually hold much humor.

Bonnie's stomach contracted in fear. People only got snowed in for months at a time back in the olden days, right? All of the sudden, one of her favorite childhood books – *The Long Winter* by Laura Ingalls Wilder – didn't seem quite as wonderful. She loved snow – she didn't want to be buried by it for months on end. There was a difference.

"We are going to be fine, too," Carmelita said with authority. "I was not feeling so well last night so I did not think to say this, but I always keep Sterno cans and a camp stove on hand in case of emergency. I can still cook for us."

"You do?" Stetson asked, surprised.

"How do you think I cooked for you last winter when the electricity was gone all day?" she asked, smiling.

"I don't know – magic?" he said, shrugging.

"I am that, too," she said and winked.

Bonnie laughed, as did everyone else. Damn, it was great to have something to laugh about. She felt a little of her panic easing in her stomach. She might not have the slightest clue of how to handle snowdrifts up to the rafters, but she wasn't alone. She didn't have to figure it out on her own.

"Now you should all go outside and celebrate Christmas, for today is Christmas Day, and you should have fun. I will ring the dinner bell when it is time to come in for breakfast."

The group discussed what could be done outside and quickly decided on sledding. The slope in the backyard that led to the forest at the edge of the clearing was apparently the perfect place to go sledding, according to Stetson. Jennifer and Bonnie hurried to change into their snowsuits from the day before while Luke and Stetson stoked the fire and opened the door to the kitchen, hoping to let the heat seep in there while Carmelita was cooking.

They met up in the backyard, Stetson pulling old-fashioned sleds out of storage in the garage rafters. Bonnie stared at hers for a moment – it looked old enough to star in a Norman Rockwell painting – and she wasn't entirely sure it'd hold together. Luke caught her look and said, "Don't worry, I spent half my childhood on these sleds. Stetson has the best sledding hill in the county, and it's right here in his backyard. Every kid around knew to come out here after a snowstorm. I promise, it'll hold up to any abuse you can throw at it."

She smiled, chagrined that her uncertainty had shone through so clearly.

"C'mon, let's take a run at this," Luke said, and held his hand out for her. She took it, her heart racing, smiling up at him. *God*, he was cute. What on earth did the town of Sawyer do to grow such handsome men? Did all of the women take Extra Cute Children Vitamins while pregnant?

"Race you to the bottom!" Stetson hollered, and threw himself onto the sled, barreling down the slope at top speed. Bonnie couldn't help it; she burst out into laughter.

They began racing each other down the slope, the snow getting packed and faster with each pass of the curled wooden sleds. The flakes continued to fall, sticking to Luke's long eyelashes and hair, somehow making him even more handsome than before. Bonnie was laughing and Stetson and Luke were razzing each other and Jennifer was breathless and laughing too, and the happiness welled up inside of Bonnie at the picture-perfect moment. If only it could continue forever…

The air rang with the striking of the dinner bell. Luke offered to pull Bonnie's sled back up the hill one last time for her and she willingly agreed. The wooden sleds may be indestructible but they were *heavy*, and her legs were tired from pushing through the snow that ranged from mid-calf to mid-thigh. It was amazing what a workout it was to go sledding. She mentally gave herself permission to eat whatever Carma was cooking, considering she'd probably just burned off all those calories and more.

They walked into the house, laughing and brushing their boots off, trying to get rid of the egregious chunks of snow before they tracked it everywhere.

"You must go to change before you sit down to eat," Carmelita said from her position over the Sterno stove. "I am not quite done cooking but called you early to have you change clothes now."

Is there anything *that gets past her? She really is magical.*

Bonnie hurried to change into her warmest clothing – sweatpants and a hoodie – in the cold of her bedroom. She looked at the fireplace longingly, but knew it didn't make sense to build a fire just for her room, when they could share the wood and the heat down in the living room.

She scurried out of her bedroom…and right into Luke in the hallway, heading back downstairs after also changing. His dark hair was damp but he'd taken the time to run a comb through it, something that Bonnie realized with a sinking feeling in her gut that she hadn't bothered to do. She shoved at her hair with her hand. She probably looked like a disaster – a homeless person in sweatpants and wild hair – and oh God, there was just *no way* he'd still be attracted to her.

Which is when he bent down and kissed her.

CHAPTER 12

LUKE

*H*E KNEW he hadn't asked her if he could kiss her and she probably wasn't expecting it, but literally running into her in the hallway, her soft curves pressing against his body for just a moment until she straightened and realize who she'd run into…

He couldn't help himself. Her dark brown hair looked delightfully mussed, as if they were just crawling out of bed after a nice, long…interlude, and he couldn't help the quick tightening of his body at the sight of her. She was so damn gorgeous.

He pulled her closer to him at the moan she let out, burying his hands into her hair, tilting her head to gain better access to her delicious mouth, his groans mingling with hers, tongues dueling, learning the feel of each other, her lips so soft and delicious under his.

Slowly, he forced himself to pull away. Some part of his mind – the part still functioning – knew that they'd been gone a long time and someone was going to send out a search party for them if they didn't get their asses downstairs.

Not to mention that Bonnie's adorable nose – was there any part of her that *wasn't* adorable? – was cold to the touch. It was freezing upstairs, although that was helpful when trying to keep certain...parts of him under control.

Her eyes fluttered open. "Hi," she said breathlessly.

"Hi," he said, grinning down at her. How was it that being around her seemed to make him perpetually happy? She was some kind of antidote to the harshness of the world he was used to dealing with.

"I think we should go downstairs," he whispered to her.

"Okay," she whispered back. "Why are we whispering?"

"I don't know," he admitted...while whispering. She burst out laughing, a joyous sound that he loved to hear. She had to be one of the most genuinely happy people that he knew.

Christmas Day passed in a whirl of fun, food, and laughter. They played the Farming Game all afternoon, gathered around the coffee table, while Carmelita watched and knitted from her perch on the couch. In an upset no one expected, Bonnie the newbie actually won.

"That's not fair!" Stetson protested. "You're not a

farmer!" She just grinned in response while ostentatiously flipping through her stacks of play money on her side of the board.

Stetson flopped back on the floor dramatically, which of course Sticks took as an invitation to give him a face bath. Stetson came up stuttering and Luke, laughing so hard his stomach hurt, leaned over and kissed Bonnie on the lips without thinking. She sucked in a quick breath of surprise but then opened her mouth beneath his kisses, allowing his tongue to dip into her mouth.

He finally pulled back and, blinking, turned towards the rest of the group. He felt like he was under the spell of a witch – a wonderful witch who'd made his heart light and his worries few.

Stets gave him a "Good for you!" grin while Jennifer had a Cheshire grin plastered across her face. She seemed pretty damn delighted with herself, and even though Luke believed her when she said that they hadn't set him and Bonnie up on purpose, he also wasn't naïve enough to think that she hadn't been doing her darnedest to push them together since then.

Bonnie smoothed at her sweatshirt, her cheeks flushed a delicious shade of pink. *She* was delicious. Luke had visions of scooping her up into his arms and carrying her up the stairs to his guest bedroom and making slow, amazing love to her all evening.

Stetson, who was busy shuffling up a pack of face cards to play Texas Hold 'Em, caught Luke's eye and winked. Luke knew that Stetson knew *exactly* what

Luke was thinking. Luke felt his own cheeks flush a little. He knew he was as obvious as a flashing neon sign, but he couldn't seem to help himself.

Bonnie, who was actually paying attention to what Stetson was doing instead of letting hormones take over her brain, protested that she'd never played that version of poker before. Stetson's eyes narrowed at her. "Yeah, but you hadn't played the Farming Game before either, so I'm thinking that beginner's luck is strong with you."

She grinned innocently. "I guess we'll just have to try it and see," she said with a shrug. Luke knew that this meant that they were on – Stetson was one of the most competitive men he'd ever met, so he knew that beating Bonnie was a point of pride by now.

He smiled to himself. It was going to be fun to see Stetson taken down a peg or two.

CHAPTER 13

BONNIE

*B*ONNIE SQUEALED in triumph as she laid down her four 2's, and everyone burst out laughing, even Stetson.

"Are you *sure* you're not sandbagging me?" Stetson asked with a wry grin as he gathered up the cards.

Jennifer took the opportunity to stand up and stretch, and light a few more candles. The snow was still continuing to fall outside, and it was growing dark earlier than normal. Luke unfolded his long legs and moved over to the fire to add a few more logs.

Bonnie simply shrugged at Stetson's question and grinned. "Sometimes, a girl's got the touch," she said, wiggling her fingers at Stetson. He laughed.

The Christmas music stopped playing – the tape must've ended – and just as Stetson opened his mouth to reply, the lights turned on, flickering for a few moments, and then staying lit. Everyone burst into laughter and cheers.

"Good job, Idaho Power!" Luke hollered and everyone laughed.

Bonnie strolled over to the windows to look into the backyard. The signs of their sledding were still evident, but many of the tracks through the snow had filled in, leaving only dips in their wake. She couldn't remember ever loving Christmas as much as she had this one, and for her, that was truly saying something.

Luke moved to stand next to her, slipping his arm around her waist, and she leaned against him. She had to admit that much of the reason for her loving this Christmas was because of this man. She'd loved spending time around her best friend again and getting to know Carmelita and Stetson better, but truly, meeting Luke was simply amazing. He leaned down to kiss her and then whispered in her ear, "Now I have no excuse to snuggle next to you on the floor again."

She snuggled further into his arms and whispered back, "Well, we could always take our sweet time going upstairs tonight…"

"I like how you think," he whispered back.

The furnace whooshed back on, sending heat throughout the house like magic. Carmelita stowed her knitting away in a basket and hurried to the kitchen to get cooking again now that she had electricity. Bonnie's stomach rumbled, reminding her that food would come in handy about now.

Stetson and Jennifer wandered over to join them

at the windows, all staring into the backyard, the snow still slowly drifting down.

"I've never seen it snow this long," Stetson said. "Usually, it comes in fits and spurts. And to think that the weatherman had said an inch!" They all chuckled at the absurdity of it.

"Remind me not to believe Channel 12 weather again," Luke said wryly. "I left my chains at home, so I don't know how long it'll be before I can get out of here. You may have me as a guest for a while." He looked down at Bonnie. "Do you have chains for your car?"

She tried not to laugh too loudly. "Umm…no. In Boise, you can get wherever you need to go sans chains. They believe in street crews and plows there."

"Hey, we can one-up that here!" Stetson chimed in. "Here, we all own our own equipment so we can be our own road crews."

Jennifer rolled her eyes. "Stetson is usually 26… until he gets behind the wheel of a 4x4 with a plow attachment on it. Then he's about four again." The love and laughter was obvious in her voice, despite her words.

"Speaking of," Stetson said, his voice getting serious, "I kept thinking that the snow would slow down, but since it just seems to keep coming, maybe we should head outside and make some passes with the plow before the snow piles even higher and we can't get out our own front door."

Luke nodded his agreement and they headed for

the stairs to change into coveralls and work boots but he casually snagged Bonnie's arm as he walked by, ignoring her startled yelp of surprise. He pulled her into the alcove for the jackets just inside the front door.

Without a word, he pointed up, and she saw mistletoe hanging by a red ribbon from the ledge.

"When we were decorating yesterday, I was using my noggin," he said with a wicked grin.

"Thinking ahead, eh? Very impressive," she said breathlessly.

"You should see what else I can do..." He dipped his head and began to kiss her and she sighed and opened her mouth to his and he buried his hands in her hair and groaned...

The moment was endless and yet it seemed to last only a moment. Or a lot of moments. Bonnie wasn't sure. She wasn't sure of much right then, except how much she was attracted to this man in front of her.

It was too soon to say *love*. She knew it. She knew that at best, this could be classified as insta-lust, although she would also say that most cases of insta-lust didn't start with trips into a bathtub mostly clothed.

But whatever she called it, she knew she wanted nothing more than to be around this man for a very long time.

And how was she supposed to make that happen?

Long after he broke away and headed upstairs to get ready to battle the snow, she stood in the alcove, lost in thought, fingering her lips as she pondered her options.

She just didn't see it. She couldn't see it. How could this be anything more than a Christmas fling? They lived 90 minutes away from each other, and it wasn't 90 minutes of straight freeway time. It was 90 minutes of winding, curving mountain roads, steep cliffs on either side, narrowing to a barely-passable-two-laner-if-you-squinted-just-right-and-didn't-allow-semis-on-there kind of road several times during the drive. She had white knuckled a couple of the corners during *daylight*. *Without* fresh snow on the road.

They would be able to see each other once, maybe twice a winter? That wasn't a relationship. It couldn't be.

And yet…the idea of heading back to Boise after the weekend was over and never seeing Luke again tore at her stomach. Tore at her heart. Made her sick. She couldn't do it. She couldn't.

But Long Valley was suspiciously short on huge accounting firms that could offer her retirement benefits and a 401k plan, and especially with her overwhelming student loan debt, she couldn't afford to simply quit.

Suddenly, Jennifer's arms were wrapping around her, pulling her close.

"Shhhh…" she whispered. "It's gonna be okay."

And it was only then that Bonnie realized that tears were soaking into Jennifer's shirt and as Jennifer gently stroked up and down her back, she melted against her, letting her frustration come out as she sobbed, the anger at the universe for showing her a glimpse of this world that she loved…and then yanking it away from her.

"Where," she snuffled, pulling back from Jennifer's arms, "is everyone else?" She swiped at her nose and eyes with the back of her hand, knowing that she looked just awful – she'd never mastered the art of crying beautifully – but also knowing that Jennifer didn't care. Jenn had cried on her couch many a time after the break-up with Paul, so she was one person who just didn't judge.

One of the *many* things that Bonnie loved about her.

"Stets and Luke went outside to play with their machines, and Carmelita is whipping up something in the kitchen that is bound to add yet even more 'pregnancy' weight to my waistline," Jennifer said with a smile. "When I give birth and have to lose all of this 'pregnancy' weight, I'm gonna be screwed.

"Anyway, why don't we get out of the coat closet and you can tell me why you're crying so hard you're hiccuping, under the mistletoe? I'm pretty sure that's against the rules of the Christmas mistletoe."

Bonnie smiled ruefully at Jennifer's joke. "You make fun of the Christmas mistletoe, but I believe in its powers!" she said sarcastically with a small laugh.

Jenn grinned at her. "See? Life is better already." They settled onto the couch, Jennifer pulling Bonnie's head down onto her lap and stroking her hair out of her face. Her lap was smaller than it used to be, now that the baby bump was taking up more space, but Bonnie didn't mind. It was such a joy to see her closest friend become a mother, and she knew she'd be a damn good one.

Slowly, haltingly, she told Jennifer the thoughts she'd just been wrestling with.

"And the dumbest part of all is, he hasn't even asked for anything more. I may be jumping the gun here. He flat-out told me that marriage wasn't for him, so long-term relationships probably aren't either. I'm being an idiot, but I don't seem to be able to help myself. I *like* him, Jenn."

She sat up and swung her legs underneath her, staring Jennifer straight in the eye.

"Dammit, a lot more than I really should, considering we just met. But I feel a spark around him that I've never felt for any guy, not even The Ass, Ryan Petersen. There's something there and I want to pursue it and see if it works out and instead, we have to just cut it short. We have to let it go, because a long-distance relationship, especially with a guy who lives in a world like this?" She gestured to the snow falling, ever falling, outside the living room window. "We can't just commute back and forth or whatever. After this weekend ends, that's it. We're done. It's finished before it's even really started."

Jennifer nodded thoughtfully, her concern written all over her face. "No, you're right. I don't know what to suggest to you, because just from this summer until now, it's been a really big adjustment for me to move to Long Valley from Boise. I miss you, of course, but I also miss being close to stores and movie theaters and plays and bars and…yeah, it's just a totally different world up here. In some ways, you're better suited for it – at least you've always loved snow and mountains and pine trees. For me, Stetson has been the only way that I've been able to cope with this change. Well, Stetson and Carma and some other friends I've met here. Some of the friendliest people in the world live up here.

"But I'd be lying my ass off to you if I said that it's only been roses and unicorns and sunshine since I moved to Long Valley. Why do you think I was so quick to invite you to come spend Christmas with me? I was *so* excited when you said yes; you have no idea." They grinned at each other and Jennifer pulled her in for another hug.

"I don't know," she said thoughtfully as they pulled apart. "I'll keep thinking about it and see if I can come up with any brilliant plans – any way to make this work for you two. Or at least let you two have a shot at a relationship."

Just then, the backdoor opened and Stetson and Luke, chatting, came into the kitchen. Jennifer craned her head around and looked through the open doorway at the two men. "Speaking of," she said softly under her breath, "there's our men now."

Bonnie's heart contracted at her phrasing, "our men." Was Luke hers? He looked through to the living room and, spotting her on the couch, grinned widely and winked.

It sure seemed like he wanted it.

But *how?*

She smiled back, determined to hide her worries. She could learn to live in the moment and not always try to plan ahead, right? And what better time to learn that trick than right now.

With a determined smile, she stood up from the couch and headed to the kitchen. It was time to live for right here, right now, and let the future take care of itself.

*T*HE NEXT FEW DAYS passed in a blur of laughter and pies and snowball fights and more kisses under the mistletoe. In fact, Luke found himself spending more time in the alcove by the front door than he'd ever expected to, but considering how much fun he was having in it, it was time well spent in his estimation.

The snowstorm – promptly called The Storm of the Century by all of the local news channels – finally abated, after covering all of Long Valley and most of central Idaho and western Oregon with anything from a few inches to a few feet of snow, depending on elevation. Luke knew that for some people, the snow had been a huge inconvenience and that it would take a good week for the county employees to dig everyone out, but he couldn't help thanking God for the snowstorm every day.

It gave him Bonnie just a little longer. Even her

boss from hell had realized that it would be next to impossible to require all of the employees to make it to work – even in Boise, some of the streets were still closed to thru traffic as the street crews worked to clear them all – so he'd reluctantly given everyone the day off until December 29th.

Which just happened to be the day after tomorrow.

A thought Luke was studiously avoiding.

He also made sure to check in with Ol' Willie occasionally, once the phone lines came back up, but as Ol' Willie crankily told him at one point, "You can damn well show back up in March. Until then, don't you worry 'bout it."

As strange as it was to wrap his mind around it, Luke knew Ol' Willie was right. They'd always struggled to find things to do with themselves in the winter, and although it was true he did always manage, it was also true that maybe he didn't need to.

Maybe he could take vacations, and the world would still keep spinning.

And *maybe*, he could take them with this beautiful woman. He grinned down at Bonnie, who had her pink tongue sticking out between her teeth, concentrating wholeheartedly on the gingerbread man she was decorating. He'd never seen anyone take gingerbread men so seriously. Carmelita baked up a dozen for them to decorate, but mostly, this had consisted of Stetson and Luke eating their gingerbread men while Jennifer and Bonnie were busy pouring their very creative souls into making gingerbread men that'd fit right in to the window of a bakery.

Except...Luke had eaten all of his cookies and was now eyeballing the one Bonnie had already decorated. It looked so damn good, and surely no one would notice a missing foot...or head...

"Don't even think about it," she said, without looking up.

"What?" he said, injecting as much innocence as he could into his voice, trying to cover up his surprise.

He looked up at Stetson, who just shrugged. "Jennifer can do it, too. It's scary."

"We women have radars when it comes to people trying to steal our hard work," Jennifer said without missing a beat. She was busy adding a frosting bowtie to her gingerbread man. "Our children are going to be so screwed..."

"Speaking of children," Bonnie said, "shouldn't you be able to tell if it's a girl or a boy by now?"

"Oh, I already know," Jennifer said breezily. "But Stetson wants to have a family party and tell everyone at once, including himself, so we were thinking we'd have a gender reveal party at the beginning of February. Are you going to come for it?"

Luke's heart restricted painfully when Bonnie looked up at him for just a moment, her question clear on her face – *are we going to be together then? Am I going to be up here for it?* – before she turned and forced a smile at Stetson. "So are you saying that your wife knows and you don't, and you aren't going crazy over that yet?"

"Nah. I'll be happy either way. As long as it looks like Jennifer and has ten fingers and ten toes, I'll be happy."

"And if it doesn't look like Jennifer?" she asked.

"Then I feel sorry for 'em already!" Stetson burst out laughing, as did everyone else.

Carmelita, God bless her soul, brought in another cinnamon roll each for him and Stetson, saving Luke from getting his fingers whacked for trying to sneak another piece of gingerbread man from Bonnie.

He dug into his cinnamon roll with a lusty sigh. He was *seriously* going to have to think about hiring a housekeeper out at his place. After a week of Carmelita's cooking, he just couldn't fathom going back to Ol' Willie's burnt stew.

"Carma, do you have a sister?" he called out after he put a bite of heaven into his mouth. He closed his eyes, savoring every morsel.

"I have a few sisters. Why do you ask?" His eyes popped open to see her standing in the doorway to the kitchen, wiping her hands on a tea towel.

"Just trying to imagine Life After Carmelita, and right now, I'm not sure I'm gonna live. I should eat an extra cinnamon roll so I can fatten up, just in case."

Blushing, Carmelita walked back into the kitchen, muttering, "Flattery gets you nowhere," under her breath as she went.

But he noticed it was only a couple of minutes

before another huge cinnamon roll appeared at his elbow, along with a refill of his coffee cup.

Apparently, the way to Carmelita's coffee was flattery and a clean mouth. After his screw-up that first day at the dining room table, he'd made sure to watch his mouth real closely around her. He noticed she'd already trained Stetson. He knew which side of his bread was buttered.

Or where the bread came from…

It was the next morning before Luke forced himself to face reality again. Today was the last day. Bonnie really was leaving. She had to go back to work the next morning, and wanted to give herself plenty of time to make the drive back.

Stetson had managed to clear out his driveway, the county road crew had managed to clear out the highway, and Boise had pretty much cleared out its streets. It should be easy driving. She should be good to go.

Looking at her, the pain lanced through him. It may be an easy drive for her, but that didn't make it easy on the heart. Suddenly, he began wishing for sheets of snow to come down from the sky, blanketing the world as far as the eye could see again, but the sky was that brilliant blue that only seemed to show up during the wintertime, when the air was clean and crisp and cold, and the world around him sparkled with the brilliance of winter.

Dammit, now Bonnie had him thinking about sparkling winters. She had turned him all poetical and shit. Didn't she realize how much she'd changed him in the last six days? Didn't she know he didn't want to be without her?

Everyone else had disappeared with murmurs of, "Better get back to it," so obviously wanting to give them a chance to say goodbye alone. Instead of laughing at their obviousness, Luke appreciated it. Because it was going to be hard enough to say goodbye, without having to do it in front of an audience.

She smiled up at him ruefully. "It seems like everyone else has left us," she said. "Our friends are short on subtlety."

"Yeah, it's one of the things I like best about them," he said with a forced joviality that sounded as wooden to his ear as it felt to his heart.

He reached out and pushed a lock of her gorgeous mahogany hair behind her ear. "I learned a new word this week," he said.

Startled at the abrupt change in conversation, she asked, "Yeah? What's that?"

"Mahogany. Your hair is mahogany. Such a better word than 'brown' or 'red.'"

The joyous laughter spilled out of her. "I…" She drew a deep breath and tried it again when she could stop laughing. "I am very proud of you," she said, mock-seriously. "Such a big word for a cowboy."

"Farmer," he corrected her.

"What?"

"I'm a farmer. The only animals I have are horses. I'm no cowboy."

She looked him up and down, assessing his Wranglers and cowboy hat and green plaid shirt. "Uh-huh," she said dryly. "You call it what you want. I'll just call you my cowboy."

My cowboy. Luke was instantly just fine with being called a cowboy.

She leaned forward and kissed him on the lips gently. "Thanks for a magical Christmas, cowboy," she whispered against his lips, and then before he could stop her or think of *how* to stop her or pull her into his arms and never let her go, she slipped into her car and drove away, red taillights disappearing into the gathering twilight.

The second time a woman in his life just drove away.

And damn, did that hurt. In a way he didn't even know pain could hurt – in his whole body. Everywhere. Even his damn pinky toes were heartbroken that she'd driven away and left him alone.

Again.

At his feet, Sticks whined pathetically.

"I know just what you mean, buddy. I know just what you mean."

CHAPTER 15

LUKE

"*J*ENNIFER, I can't stand it anymore. I need you to tell me how to sell my farm."

"What?!" She stared at him, wide-eyed with surprise.

"I miss her too much," he said, striding around Stetson's living room, waving his hands as he went. Past the fireplace that had kept them warm. Past the couch where they'd snuggled late at night. "These weekends together, and then not seeing each other again for days, or even weeks at a time...I can't live without her anymore, Jenn, I just can't. I used to think that marriage wasn't for me, but I used to be an idiot. I'm gonna sell my farm and move to Boise and...well, I'll work at C-A-L Ranch or something. Something!" He slumped onto the couch, and just stared at Jennifer, pain vibrating off him in thick waves. Retail wouldn't *kill* him, right?

Oh God, he didn't want to sell his farm. He loved it with all of his heart and soul. He'd given up so much for that farm – worked so hard through the spring and into the fall to make it a success. But…

He couldn't *live* without Bonnie. Coming together, being torn back apart again, over and over…

Yeah, Skype was wonderful, and sure, they had it easier than people living on the other side of the planet from each other.

But he wanted to wake up in the morning to find her by his side.

He wanted to come home at night and have the lights on in the house. Have someone there to greet him, someone to care about him.

He wanted to lean over and kiss her whenever he damn well pleased.

He most especially wanted *her*. However, whenever, wherever he could. He was sure that if he had to say goodbye to Bonnie one more time, his heart was going to be torn to shreds.

And if that meant giving up his farm, so be it. Jennifer had been in real estate and banking for a long time. She'd know what to do, how much he could ask for, who to list it with.

This whole thing was her damn fault for introducing them, so she could surely help him figure out a way to make it happen.

With the snow melting and spring planting about to begin, it was a tough time to sell a farm – he'd have to plant what he always did and just hope that a buyer wanted to buy acres of wheat.

He didn't know how long it would take to sell his farm, so he didn't dare let it sit fallow and then not have a crop to harvest that fall, if the farm was still hanging on like a noose around his neck. His yearly payment on the bank loan came due every fall after harvest, and if he was still stuck with it at that point, if he didn't have a harvest to sell, he wouldn't be able to make the payment.

No, he wouldn't let himself think that. He *had* to get rid of it, no matter how much that hurt, or what kind of hit he took on the price.

"Wow. I knew it was hard for you two to be apart, but I never considered you selling your farm." Jennifer said the words softly and he knew that she knew just what he was suggesting here.

Knew what a huge sacrifice this was.

But Bonnie was worth it. Bonnie was worth *anything*.

"I don't want to. I offered to pay off Bonnie's student loans and then she could move to Long Valley, but she's right – it's more than just her student loans. She needs money for her car payment and insurance and cell phone and food," his lips quirked slightly at that, "and so she insists on having, you know, a real job.

"So if I can't get her here, I'll move there. Surely C-A-L Ranch would love to hire someone like me, even if I've never worked a cash register in my life. I know more than those high school kids anyway."

"I've been working on a plan, Luke, tell me what you think…"

CHAPTER 16

BONNIE

*J*ENNIFER SLID THE KEY into the lock for the business and swung the front door open wide. "C'mon in," she said, gesturing with her hand to the office space in front of her, her stomach leading the way into the office. Jenn had somehow made swallowing a basketball look amazing. "It's a little brisk in here, but I haven't had the heat turned over into my name yet, so I can't turn it on. You'll just have to imagine it being warmer in here."

Bonnie smiled at her, forcing happiness into it, walking into the office. It was the end of another all-too-short weekend in Long Valley, and honestly, Bonnie was having a hard time concentrating on what Jennifer was saying. She just couldn't get her mind to look past the fact that she was about to say goodbye to Luke.

Again.

For the millionth time, she was going to drive away and cry as she went, which she was pretty sure was illegal, considering it was hard to see the road with tears in her eyes, but waiting for the tears to abate...

Well, she just didn't have years to sit in a parking lot and wait for that to happen.

Speaking of, where *was* Luke? She tried to listen to Jennifer's excited plans for her new accounting office in downtown Sawyer, but quite frankly, her heart just wasn't in it. Luke had said he'd be right behind them, but it'd been at least 20 minutes.

She surreptitiously checked her watch.

Okay, 16 minutes.

But still!

She needed to get all of the time in with him that she could, before she had to hit the road again.

Jennifer showed Bonnie the nursery, a small room off to the side that was ready and waiting for the baby's birth, decorated beautifully as always. Jenn was so talented when it came to interior decorating.

Where is Luke?

The sound of a bell jingling had Bonnie heading for the front area. She wasn't sure if Jennifer had even been talking when she walked away and she was probably going to have to apologize for being rude later, but being apart from Luke for...*checking*...19 minutes was about 19 minutes too long in her estimation.

She came around the corner to find...

Luke with a box in his hands? Why was there a box in his hands? And what was…

The world slowed and then stopped as she saw the glint of light off the diamond.

On the ring.

In the box.

There were tears then, streaming down her face, and Bonnie didn't know whether to throw herself into his arms and cry, "YEESSSS!" for the whole world to hear, or throw herself into his arms and just cry.

"Luke, I can't…we can't. Where will we live?" She kept dashing at the tears on her cheeks with the backs of her hands but the flow was never-ending.

She walked slowly towards him, her eyes flicking back and forth between his eyes and his box. It was a silver band and a gorgeous princess-cut diamond and…

How did he know that's what I wanted?!

And

Oh God, why are you torturing me?

"I need an accounting partner, you know," Jennifer said behind her. Bonnie whirled around and for the first time, noticed a second desk.

Two desks.

Jennifer held up a nameplate and through the blur of her tears, she saw *Bonnie Patterson-Nash* engraved on it.

"Yes!" she cried, throwing herself at Luke.

"Yes to which question?" Luke asked, his arms

wrapping around her, staring down at her, his dark chocolate eyes still a little worried, a little unsure.

"Yes to *both*!"

He picked her up then, pulling her against his chest, the panic in his eyes fading away, swinging her around and around.

"Yes, I will marry you, Luke Nash!" And he kissed her, and the moment was endless and yet it seemed to last only a moment. Or a lot of moments. Bonnie wasn't sure. She wasn't sure of much right then, except how much she loved this man in front of her.

"I love you, Luke," she breathed against his lips.

Jennifer said something as she slipped past them and headed outside, but Bonnie didn't hear her. Her world had narrowed to this gorgeous man in front of her.

"I love you, Bonnie Rae Patterson," Luke breathed against her lips. "I can't wait to start our life together."

Which sounded just like heaven.

❄

Quick Author's Note

GOSH, I sure hope you enjoyed *Blizzard of Love*! Although it is the shortest story in my Long Valley series, I'll confess that Luke and Bonnie are still one of my favorites. 🤍

And, as is true of all of my books, *Blizzard* is just

the beginning. Every one of my books all take place in Long Valley, Idaho, which means that you'll see Bonnie and Luke pop in and out of future books. You'll never truly have to say goodbye.

The first book in the Long Valley series is the love story between Stetson and Jennifer (with a starring role by Carmelita, of course!) in *Accounting for Love*, and if you haven't checked that out yet, you should!

But just in case you've already read *Accounting for Love* and you're wanting more, then you should absolutely check out the next book in the Long Valley word: Wyatt's story in *Arrested by Love*. You'll finally find out why Wyatt and Declan couldn't be there for Christmas, and why Stetson was so angry with them both.

You'll never guess the truth, I promise, because in Wyatt's world, mistakes are a part of life, and redemption is a hard-won battle...

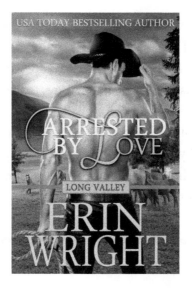

<u>Arrested by Love</u>

He's a fighter, not a lover...

Two years ago, Wyatt Miller lost his family to a drunk driver. His heart broken, he slowly put the pieces of his shattered life back together. Running his thousand-acre ranch from dawn till dusk helps him forget about his broken heart. When he stops a drunk from getting behind the wheel one night, he ends up in a bloody fight...and then behind bars.

She keeps men in line, but has a soft heart...

Abby Connelly takes her work at the Long Valley Jail seriously. She has no dreams of marriage, children, or white-picket fences. All she wants is to do her job and please the only family she has left, her father. But the moment rugged and wounded Wyatt Miller walks into her jail, Abby realizes her heart might just have a change of plans...

But small towns have a way of holding onto big grudges. Wyatt and Abby have an uphill fight to overcome the bad blood between the Miller and Connelly families.

Because redemption never comes easy...

❄

Read on for a taste of *Arrested*...

WYATT MILLER WANDERED down the snack aisle of the Mr. Petrol's at 11:30 at night. Nothing like trying to find dinner in the aisles of a convenience store. Did onion rings and beef jerky count as a balanced diet? He could consider the onion rings to be his vegetables, and the beef jerky to be his protein.

He grimaced. Some days, living in a small town really sucked, like when grocery stores prided themselves on being "open late" – all the way until nine at night.

He pulled Lay's Salt & Vinegar off the display.

Look, more vegetables.

He wasn't sure a dietician would approve, but then again, there was almost nothing in this convenience store that a dietician would approve of. He really should just drive to Franklin and go grocery shopping there, but that was 30 minutes away and he just didn't feel like it. When he died, his headstone was going to read, "Too lazy to drive to Franklin; died of a heart attack from eating junk food from Mr. Petrol's."

Just then, a vehicle pulled up outside. Well, "pulled up" made it sound like the driver was in control of their actions, but as Wyatt watched, his bag of chips forgotten in his hands, he saw the Jeep stop *just* in time to keep from crashing through the front windows of the convenience store.

Oh shit.

He knew that Jeep. There was only one orange camo Jeep in the valley.

The driver's side door swung open and out swaggered Richard. Wyatt couldn't tell if Richard was swaggering because he was so arrogant and full of himself – always a possibility – or because he was drunk – definitely another possibility.

Wyatt reminded himself to breathe in, and then out. And then repeat it all over again. He couldn't react the way he wanted to – a punch to the face – so he needed to just stay calm. That's what everyone would tell him, anyway.

He knew that. It was a matter of remembering that. And doing that.

No matter how good a punch to Richard's face would feel.

Richard stumbled into the store and from two aisles over, Wyatt could smell the fumes rolling off him.

Drunk it was.

Richard managed to make his way over to the beer case without taking out an end-cap display, nothing short of a miracle really, and snagged a 24-pack of Budweiser.

A 24-pack? Really? When you're already this wasted?

Wyatt was having a hard time breathing again and he realized that he'd smashed the bag of chips in his hands into a tiny ball, chips spilling onto the floor from the busted seams of the bag. Richard didn't seem to notice the noise, though, swinging the 24-pack up onto the counter and swiping his debit card moments later.

Breathe in, breathe out.

Wyatt was hoping that at any moment, the cashier would stop him. Surely, he'd realize that giving Richard more beer at this point was a truly awful idea.

Right?

Richard took his beer and began stumbling towards the door.

The cashier wasn't going to stop him. Wyatt could feel the rage begin to boil up inside of him.

"Why did you sell him that beer?!" The words burst out of Wyatt like gunfire. He couldn't stop himself from asking any more than he could stop himself from breathing.

"Dude, do you know who that is?" the cashier responded with a shrug.

"Of *course* I know who that is," Wyatt ground out.

"Well, my probation is almost up. Just a month

more and I'm out of the system. I'm not pissing off the judge's son."

That was it. Wyatt threw the mangled bag of chips to the floor and sprinted for the door. He wasn't about to stand by and let Richard take someone's life because he happened to share genetic material with the only judge in town. Oh *hell* no.

He burst out the front door of Mr. Petrol's. Richard had finally managed to get his key into the ignition and turn it. Wyatt grabbed the door handle and yanked it open.

"Whaddya want, killer?" Richard slurred, blearily focusing his eyes on Wyatt.

"Hello, brother. Nice to see you again." Wyatt pulled back his fist and planted it squarely in the middle of Dick's nose.

❄

Available at your favorite retailer or library – pick your copy up today!

ALSO BY ERIN WRIGHT

~ LONG VALLEY ~

Accounting for Love

Blizzard of Love

Arrested by Love

Returning for Love

Christmas of Love

Overdue for Love

Bundle of Love

Lessons in Love

Baked with Love

Bloom of Love (2021)

Holly and Love (TBA)

Banking on Love (TBA)

Sheltered by Love (TBA)

Conflicted by Love (TBA)

~ FIREFIGHTERS OF LONG VALLEY ~

Flames of Love

Inferno of Love

Fire and Love

Burned by Love

~ MUSICIANS OF LONG VALLEY ~

Strummin' Up Love

Melody of Love (TBA)

Rock 'N Love (TBA)

Rhapsody of Love (TBA)

~ SERVICEMEN OF LONG VALLEY ~

Thankful for Love (2021)

Commanded to Love (TBA)

Salute to Love (TBA)

Harbored by Love (TBA)

ABOUT ERIN WRIGHT

USA Today Bestselling author Erin Wright has worked every job under the sun, including library director, barista, teacher, website designer, and ranch hand helping brand cattle, before settling into the career she's always dreamed about: Author.

She still loves coffee, doesn't love the smell of cow flesh burning, and has embarked on the adventure of a lifetime, traveling the country full-time in an RV. (No one has died yet in the confined 250-square-foot space – which she considers a real win – but let's be real, next week isn't looking so good…)

Find her updates on ErinWright.net, where you can sign up for her newsletter along with the requisite pictures of Jasmine the Writing Cat, her kitty cat muse and snuggle buddy extraordinaire.

Wanna get in touch?
www.erinwright.net
erin@erinwright.net

Or reach out to Erin on your favorite social media platform:

facebook.com/AuthorErinWright

twitter.com/erinwrightlv

pinterest.com/erinwrightbooks

goodreads.com/erinwright

bookbub.com/profile/erin-wright

instagram.com/authorerinwright

Printed in the USA
CPSIA information can be obtained
at www.ICGtesting.com
LVHW020201291123
765250LV00014B/85